The Nightmare Rally

The Nightmare Rally

Pierre Castex

*

TRANSLATED FROM THE FRENCH BY
HUGH SHELLEY

Abelard-Schuman
LONDON NEW YORK TORONTO

Original title: *Le Rallye Fantastique*

Library of Congress Catalogue Card Number 65:11385
First published in U.S.A. 1965

LONDON
Abelard-Schuman
Limited
8 King Street WC2

NEW YORK
Abelard-Schuman
Limited
6 West 57 Street

TORONTO
Abelard-Schuman
Canada Limited
896 Queen St. West

GLOSSARY OF TERMS UNFAMILIAR TO AMERICAN READERS

Argus de l'Automobile	automobile trade paper
arrivée	FINISH
bonnet	hood
boot	trunk
bottom gear	low gear
breakdown lorry	tow truck
brewer's lorry	beer truck
car-park	parking lot
chemist's	drugstore
chicane	obstacle
coachbuilder	body repairman
commercial traveller	traveling salesman
concièrge	janitor
distributor	ignition
flat	apartment
Gare de Lyon	Lyon railroad station (in Paris)
gendarme	policeman
gentles	maggots
junction	intersection
képi	hat worn by French policeman
lorry	truck
notes	bills
oilskin	slicker
paraffin	benzine
petrol	gasoline
point duty	traffic duty
roundabout	traffic circle *or* carousel
saloon (car)	sedan
signal	winker
spanner	wrench
tyre	tire
tote window	betting window
underground	subway
van	truck
verge	siding
windscreen (wiper)	windshield (wiper)
wing	fender

❋ ❋ 1 ❋ ❋

WITH A LONG LOAF OF BREAD tucked under his arm, Gendarme Tropinet stood waiting without any particular hurry for a break in the traffic so that he could cross the National Highway 4. It was the crucial hour. On this late May afternoon, hundreds of suburbanites had just been let out of their offices and factories and werc rushing away to their country cottages. Tropinet, himself, was looking forward to exchanging the parish of Ormesson for that of Plessis-Trévise, where he lovingly tended half an acre of garden. He was confident that he would return from his expedition with his first lettuce of the year . . . Musing thus, he was waiting patiently at the junction of the N. 4 highway and the D. 125 road, when . . .

The coral-red Dauphine was speeding towards Paris. It was a hundred yards from the junction. At the same moment a brewer's lorry appeared, going in the direction of Noiseau. The driver conscientiously pulled up at the stop sign. It was all quite straightforward. As an expert, Gendarme Tropinet admired the result of scrupulous observation of the Highway Code: on approaching a main road from a secondary one, the lorry stopped for a moment until the road was clear and it could proceed.

"I don't know what happened," Tropinet said later to a colleague of his who had to make the report, as he (Tropinet) was not on duty at the time.

Tropinet could not understand it, but for the good name of the *gendarmerie* let it be made clear that he was not the only one.

Did the driver of the Dauphine think that the lorry driver was going to ignore the stop sign? He slammed on his brakes and pulled his wheel hard over to the left. The car clung angrily to the road, but swerved across the yellow line, on the other side of which a double line of motorized suburbanites was streaming past in the opposite direction.

The Dauphine seemed to bounce off the left wing of a Peugeot 403 which crashed into a Citroën 2 CV and sent it flying into the ditch with three other cars after it. The coral Dauphine seemed to have gone quite crazy: it spun round twice, shot off to the right, just missed the lorry, jumped into a field by the side of the road and ended up with its nose in a pond.

Surprise and fright made Gendarme Tropinet drop his loaf of bread. By the time an automatic reflex had made him bend down and pick it up, it was all over. The stream of suburbanites had been halted. Men were running to assist those in the accident. Drivers were being helped out of their crumpled cars. Tropinet dashed down towards the pond. The lorry driver was there already, standing up to his knees in the water, trying to open the door of the Dauphine. The driver, apparently unhurt, was trying to help him from inside. Tropinet joined in and soon the man was able to get back on dry land.

The first effect of a road accident is to produce a crowd of curious spectators at a previously deserted spot. The fields on each side of the road junction miraculously sprouted hundreds of gaping onlookers. Then the police cars arrived. There was no sign of an ambulance. The monster pile-up which had prevented Gendarme Tropinet from picking the first lettuce of the season resulted in no more than a few bumps and scratches. The uninjured drivers who had been flung into the ditch crowded round the author of their misfortunes. A whole Greek chorus started up:

"Who's going to pay for my damaged wing?"

"And my rear wheels?"

"My boot is smashed in!"

Still dazed by his fantastic caper, and attacked from all sides, the driver of the coral Dauphine kept saying, like an automaton:

"My name is Antoine Gavard. Born in Paris in 1930. Employed by the World Health Organization . . .My insurance company . . . All claims . . . Don't worry . . ."

The police took down the particulars. The owners of the damaged cars watched. The onlookers made their comments. Passing drivers slowed down and shuddered . . .

Half an hour went by like this; then suddenly there was a tremendous clanging and clattering from the direction of a secondary road leading to Le Plessis . . . Police and onlookers all turned towards it. A sort of prehistoric monster was advancing on the road junction. It was a fierce red vehicle with a little crane cocked up on the back like a squirrel's tail.

"What on earth's that?" growled the police sergeant in charge.

Gendarme Tropinet gave a little cough.

"It's the breakdown lorry you asked for, Sarge. All the local garages were busy, so I got onto the Garage de l'Avenir at Plessis. He doesn't really do wrecks, but he said he'd come along."

The monster clattered to a standstill beside the little group of police and stranded motorists. The driver of the contraption switched off his engine and jumped down, followed by a young mechanic.

"Auguste Bricard, Garage de l'Avenir," was all he said to introduce himself.

He was a tough, stocky little man, bald as an egg. Two compelling blue eyes stared out of a cheerful pink countenance.

The sergeant grimaced, nodded towards the red breakdown lorry and, referring to the cars lying about the field and the ditch, said doubtfully:

"Can you cope with this?"

Auguste Bricard gave a start. His cheeks suffused with rage. He opened his mouth to reply in no uncertain fashion, but suddenly restrained himself. Instead he turned to his mechanic, who was surveying the scene with a quizzical smile, and said:

"Come on, Robert. Let's go and see what it's all about!"

The two of them went off, followed by the owners of the damaged cars.

"Let's have a look at this," Bricard murmured as he took hold of the left front wheel of a Peugeot 403 that had been sent into the ditch by the collision, and whose owner feared that the steering had been damaged.

The man stood with his mouth open, waiting for the garage proprietor's diagnosis.

"She'll do," Bricard finally muttered as he straightened up.

The man was already sighing with relief as Bricard continued:

"You can drive off . . . if your home isn't too far. Take it easy and get your own garage to have a look at your front suspension . . ."

With precision, efficiency and speed, Bricard and

his assistant went from one car to the next, walked all round them, appraised them like a couple of dealers at a cattle market, and then unhesitatingly put their finger on the damaged part, felt it, started up the engine and listened . . . In a quarter of an hour all the piled-up vehicles which had turned the lucerne field into a scrap yard had been retowed to the road.

The red breakdown lorry proved twice that you must not judge by appearances. It pulled two vehicles out of the ditch as though they were toys . . .

Then Monsieur Gavard came up.

"If you've finished dealing with my victims, perhaps you'd have a look at my Dauphine . . . I've just had a glance at it. The engine compartment has been smashed in . . . I can't tell what's happened to the front . . . It's in the mud."

They walked across the road.

"You've been lucky," Bricard said to the motorist, looking at the tyre marks on the road and in the field that traced the Dauphine's wild career. It was lucky you came to rest in the pond and not against that oak tree beside it . . ."

"She's sinking in the mud," Monsieur Gavard pointed out gloomily. "When they got me out of her, the water was only up to the rear-door frame."

Once again the breakdown lorry came into its own. Even the police sergeant, who had been so contemptuous a moment before, could not restrain a whistle of admiration as he saw the scarlet monster's mechanical winch effortlessly pull the Dauphine out of its mud-hole.

"Your equipment isn't . . . er . . . it isn't much to look at," he said, "but it works. That's useful to know. When the occasion demands, I'll be glad to call on your services . . ."

This time it was Auguste Bricard who scowled. "For

heaven's sake, don't!" he exclaimed. "I loathe this sort of work. I only came because none of my colleagues were available. Tropinet insisted. He even threatened to stop letting me have his maggots, as he does each time we meet out fishing together. Perhaps you didn't know he bred his own? They work wonders!"

The winch slowly drew the Dauphine out of the pond.

The little car was soon on terra firma. They went up to it. Monsieur Gavard turned pale. The roof was all lumps and bumps and looked as though an elephant had been playing with it. The front end had been pushed back a good foot.

"She's certainly taken a bashing!" said Bricard.

Gavard nodded. He had forgotten his fright, his capers, the pile-up and all the trouble the accident was going to cause him. He had eyes only for his car.

"Do you think she can be repaired?" he asked anxiously.

The garage proprietor made a doubtful gesture that meant "Nothing's impossible . . . even with cars!" But all he said was:

"Where do you want me to take her?"

"I don't really know what I ought to do with her," Gavard began. "You see, I use a garage near the Gare de Lyon. That's where I keep her when I'm in Paris. They do my repairs for me as well . . . But I don't know if it's worth my while paying tow charges all the way to Paris . . . What do you think?"

It was quite obvious that Auguste Bricard had no views at all on the subject. He could not care less about Gavard's little problems. However, as he was a decent chap, he suggested:

"I suppose I can put her in a corner of my garage, where she wouldn't be in the way. Then your man can come and fetch her when you've made up your mind . . ."

Gavard thought for a second and accepted the offer.

"If it wouldn't be a nuisance, I'd like to come with you," he added. "I've finished with the police. When we're back at your place, you can take a closer look at the car and estimate the cost of repairing her . . . Then I'll have something to go on . . ."

Five minutes later things had returned to normal at the junction. The onlookers had dispersed. The police had gone back to headquarters. On the shoulder of the road, fragments of broken glass, the only remains of the accident, winked in the last rays of the setting sun. Once again the cars streamed past without a break . . .

The Garage de l'Avenir had been established by its founder, Auguste Bricard, whom his friends called the Crankhandle, or just the Crank, in a little back street in Plessis, right on the outskirts of town and not far from those last few fields that still resist the all-devouring encroachments of suburbia. The place consisted of an old barn with a little house stuck on to one side of it. Bricard had transformed it into a garage simply by putting up a sign and, of course, by employing his indisputable talent as a mechanic. A bench, a lathe and a drill stood in one corner of the huge building filled with rusty engines that would never go again, bits of body work that were due to go to the junk yard—"any moment now", as the Crank announced daily—two or three cars badly in need of repair and, inevitably, a strange-looking object, brightly painted and bearing on its side a black numeral on a white circle—a racing sports car.

For apart from the local trade, Bricard included among his faithful customers a number of racing motorists and rally drivers, who thought nothing of coming from the other side of Paris for him to tune their precious vehicles.

When Monsieur Gavard climbed out of the breakdown lorry, his first impression of the Garage de l'Avenir was not very enthusiastic. Everyone else visiting that great glory hole for the first time had the same reaction. Almost immediately, however, he spotted the little sports car that stood out like a rose among the thorns in these surroundings. He started to walk round it and have a look while Bricard was doing some skilful manoeuvering in the narrow Rue Bon-Repos in order to bring the breakdown lorry and the Dauphine into the garage.

"What is it?" he asked Robert, the mechanic, who was standing nearby.

"An English Austin. It belongs to Gentien . . ."

As Gavard did not seem any the wiser, he added:

"Gentien, the racing driver. He's given it to the Crank to tune up. He's going in for the Monte Carlo Rally."

Gavard did not try to hide his astonishment. That a man like this Gentien, who was obviously a somebody, should entrust his car to the Garage de l'Avenir impressed him considerably. But "the Crank" . . .?

"I should have said Monsieur Bricard," Robert explained.

It was a tradition that went back thirty years to the time when the young Auguste Bricard was first with Bugatti. When people spoke to the garage proprietor, they called him "Monsieur Auguste Bricard". When they were talking about him, they said "the Crank". The tradition was scrupulously observed by both friends and clients. Bricard did not consider his nickname offensive, far from it. He had earned it through hard work and experience with Bugatti, Alfa-Romeo, Amédée Gordini, in the manufacturers' garages, in the

Le Mans Twenty-four Hours' Grand Prix d'Endurance, and the Mille Miglia. "The Crank" was a decoration awarded him out of the affection and respect of his peers.

"If people call me the Crank behind my back, that's fine," he would say with a twinkle. "Then there's no risk of mixing me up with all the other Bricards in the world . . . But when they are talking to my face, there's no danger of a mistake . . . so they might as well say Bricard. I prefer it . . ."

Robert helped the Crank to park the Dauphine in a corner of the barn and then went off laughing. The Crank watched him with a smile, then turned to Gavard, who was just waiting for attention.

"He's nineteen. With all the enthusiasm and impatience of youth. Wonderful, isn't it!"

At last the garage proprietor bent over the Dauphine, or, to be more exact, the wreck of the Dauphine, and muttered:

"Let's scc what you could do with this contraption . . ."

He proceeded to examine it with minute care.

When he had finished, he said by way of a preamble:

"You don't know me. You therefore have no reason to believe me . . . I expect you're like most people; think garage owners are a lot of crooks . . . I must tell you, however, that even if you were to go down on bended knees, I'd refuse to work on your car . . ."

Gavard opened his mouth, but the Crank did not give him the chance to speak.

"No. I don't say no to work. Only I've enough on hand, and the sort of work your car needs doesn't appeal to me. The body work's all bashed in, so the door panels will have to be hammered out . . . There's the front suspension to repair . . . the whole of the steering . . . and I don't know what else. And I've no axe to grind! Anyway, your own garage will confirm what I tell you . . ."

Monsieur Gavard, as gloomy as Napoleon after Waterloo, groaned. Being no mechanical expert, he did not contest the evidence: his Dauphine was in a sorry state. He realized that the repairs would cost a tidy sum. But exactly how much would they come to?

"Somewhere round 3,000 francs."

The motorist reeled under the blow.

"Three thousand?" he moaned faintly. "Are you *sure?*"

"Within 300 francs, yes," said the Crank—adding, as a Parthian shot, "and those 300 are more likely than not to be on the wrong side!"

This last blow finished Gavard, who just stood looking dumbly and bitterly at the coral Dauphine.

"It couldn't be worse," he said eventually, "I have only liability insurance and the accident was entirely my own fault . . . I live in Geneva where I work for the World Health Organization. Every month I come to Paris for a few days . . . I was working until very late last night. I barely slept. I was exhausted when I took the wheel . . . That's obviously the explanation of that idiotic reflex action that made me brake and pull over the wheel when I saw the lorry . . ."

"You should never drive when you're not fit," agreed the Crank.

"She's in very good condition . . . only 30,000 miles," Gavard mused, thinking of something else. "I bought her new two years ago . . . What is her price on the second-hand market?"

The Crank did not reply. Being a decent chap, he went over to a sort of wooden hut in one corner of the barn, which he called his office, to look for the *Argus de l'Automobile*. After quite a while he unearthed it.

According to the *Argus*, Monsieur Gavard's Dauphine was worth 4,200 francs.

The driver-in-distress did some rapid mental arithmetic. Four thousand two hundred minus 3,000 leaves 1,200.

"If I have 1,200 francs left after paying the minimum cost of repairs, I could make a deposit on a car just like this one before she was smashed up . . . It always makes one feel uneasy to drive a vehicle that has been in an accident; you don't feel safe . . ."

The Crank reassured him. If the repairs were done thoroughly, the Dauphine would give him no trouble . . .

"Suppose I sold her as she is," he asked point-blank, "how much could I hope to get for her?"

"A scrap yard would give you 800 francs for her—maybe a thousand."

Suddenly the Crank's attitude changed. He might not care about the idea of repairing the car, but the thought of buying it for scrap seemed to interest him. Gavard looked him in the eye.

"It strikes me that a thousand francs would be the minimum price," he said. "The dealers would make a handsome profit on that."

"Don't forget she's a wreck," the Crank reminded him, looking down modestly at his feet. "A scrap merchant would take her off your hands precisely in order to make a handsome profit."

"Would you care to make an offer?"

The garage owner's bright eyes rested on him. There was an almost boyish twinkle in them.

"All right," he said, laughing, "I'm a rotten businessman. You've guessed right. I'm in the market for her . . . She's what I want. I don't like haggling: let's put our cards on the table. A scrap yard would give you a maximum of a thousand francs. You can check on that easily enough. Look in the Classified Directory and telephone two or three of them . . . I'm offering you 1,200!"

It was Gavard's turn to change his attitude. This sudden interest in the wreck seemed suspicious. The garage owner must have sensed a bargain. This "Crank" with his jovial manner was trying to trick him . . . He was just about to get down to some hard bargaining when along came a pink-and-white lady of about fifty. This was Madame Bricard, who had arrived to fetch her husband . . . It was getting late. Gavard suddenly realized he was exhausted. It had been a most upsetting day. And he was hungry . . .

"Come on," said the Crank, taking him by the arm, "we'll finish the conversation over a nice bowl of hot soup. You need something to set you up and you've still to get to Paris. While we're eating, I'll explain to you why I want that car."

Gavard let himself be persuaded, reproaching himself for not being sharp and admitting to himself that after a second plate of soup he would be capable of letting the Dauphine go for 500. As he followed the garage owner, he hoped that the latter would neither take advantage of his hunger nor of his weakened condition.

✻ ✻ 2 ✻ ✻

As robert daroux strode along to work next morning he sadly reflected on his great ambition in life: to become a racing driver!

He had been dreaming about it for ten years, ever since the moment when Auguste Bricard had yielded to his wife's pressure and set up on his own as the proprietor of the Garage de l'Avenir. With the other boys in the district, Robert had started hanging around the barn. They had gradually grown bolder. At home, his parents expressed their astonishment that a motor engineer should be so bold as to set up in business right off the main road, in the very heart of Le Plessis, on a street that never saw more than three cars a day. His parents shook their heads and prophesied certain bankruptcy . . . By then the boys had chosen the Rue Bon-Repos as their headquarters. They waited for the bankruptcy, they were longing to see it, wondering what sort of a strange animal it could be . . . Besides, Monsieur Bricard was nice. He didn't shout at them. He had bright eyes and a pink face, he was always cheerful and he never stopped whistling between his teeth. Madame Bricard was pink, too, with wonderful white hair, and often gave you a sweet. A week after moving in, Monsieur Bricard had a visit which excited not only the children but the whole district. A little low-slung car, squatting on its wheels like a spider, turned into the quiet back street where nothing ever happened. Its engine droned like a bee on a windowpane. It dived into the garage, followed by every boy in the district. The driver, who was a great lanky fellow, heaved himself out of the cockpit and slapped Monsieur Bricard on the back. Soon they were both leaning over the engine. Monsieur Bricard called the man in the little racing car "Hamel." And Serge Rivois, who was Robert's best friend and read the sports pages of his father's newspaper, told the other boys that this man Hamel was a champion, he had seen his name in the headlines. After Hamel, other champions appeared, each time at the wheel of noisy, garish-looking machines . . . It struck the people of Le Plessis that a man capable of servicing racing cars ought to be able to repair their old buses. If Bricard had wanted, the Garage de l'Avenir could have turned into a great edifice of reinforced concrete with a workshop employing a dozen mechanics and a snazzy office for the boss. But that wasn't what Auguste Bricard wanted.

"I've got my position on the side of the track," he said cheerfully. "I like watching the others race . . . A little tinkering and a spot of fishing is enough for me."

And he kept peacefully and happily to this schedule. Once a year, in June, he shut up the garage. Monsieur Bricard took a week's holiday. He got his old Citroën, Rosalie, out of the back of the barn and, with Madame Adèle Bricard in her Sunday best enthroned beside him, he set off for Le Mans. "The Twenty-four Hours race takes me a week," he would explain. "Besides, it takes me four days on the road to get there and back." And he'd laugh while Adèle cast up her eyes in despair: she always complained that Auguste refused to repair Rosalie properly or to exchange her. For the Crank, who was so punctilious about other people's cars, neglected his own abominably. He did so out of a kind of devilry. He loved seeing people's horrified expressions when he told them he had been driving for six months with a loose connecting rod. He would then explain amiably that this was not a *major* disaster. All he had to do was to disconnect the spark plug corresponding to the affected cylinder so as to take it out of the circuit . . . You could go for hundreds of miles like that so long as you drove carefully, of course . . .

"The cobbler's child's always the worst shod," he would say, "but they get by: they learn to hop on one foot."

Robert Daroux was nine years old when Bricard came to the Rue Bon-Repos. He lived quite near with his parents in a little cottage in the fields. He and his friend Serge were the Crank's best audience. He had grown up with the names of the great champions tinging in his ears: Nuvolari, Sommer, Wimille—even Fangio, whom Bricard had known in his early days with Gordini. One day when his parents were debating his future, Robert had announced: "I'm going to be a racing driver!"

There were immediate expostulations. And when the boy insisted, Madame Daroux had been almost in tears, wailing that it wasn't a proper profession and that they all got killed. Monsieur Daroux had said nothing, but the next day he went to see the Crank. He wanted to have a serious talk with the garage owner.

"He wants to race," Monsieur Daroux said. "He dreams of nothing but cylinders, pistons and camshafts!"

"Let him take his Mechanic's Certificate," was the substance of the advice he received from the one responsible for the birth of this vocation. "If he still has the bug after that, I'll take him on: I need a hand. As for racing, don't panic: when I was his age, and a lot older, it was all I lived for . . . And I'm still here!"

So it came about that, a few years later, Robert Daroux went to work for the Crank. When he arrived at the garage with his first pair of dungarees under his arm, Auguste Bricard said to him seriously:

"You've got your Certificate. You know quite a few things, but you don't know everything . . . Without exaggerating, I think I can turn you into a pretty good mechanic. When I reckon that I can let you out in public without blushing for you, we'll both put on our best bib and tucker and go and call on my old pals in every racing spot in France. They'll take you on, all right: you've the Crank's word for it. It'll be a first step up the ladder. If you've got what it takes—and if you're lucky—you may one day be a racing driver. But, I'm warning you, it'll take a long time: you'll have a lot of setbacks, a lot of disappointments . . . Do you think you'll be able to stick to it?"

"I trust you," was all Robert said. "I'll be able to stick to it."

Robert arrived at the garage at eight in the morning, his usual time. He generally found the doors still shut. Auguste Bricard liked lazing in bed. "It's in the morning when I'm curled up nice and snug between the sheets that I have my best ideas," he claimed. Madame Bricard bristled at this claim of his, stating categorically that she had never seen anyone meditate like her husband. "Bricard," she said, "thinks with his eyes closed, making a sort of noise that is exactly like a snore." To Robert's amazement, he found the doors of the garage wide open. And what was more, there was the Crank himself, freshly shaved and bright of eye, whistling away to himself as he circled round the wreck of the coral Dauphine.

Catching his mechanic's astonished glance, Bricard said with a twinkle:

"You see, you second-rate grease monkey—I can get up early, and even not go to bed at all when the job demands it. When I was with Gordini, and not so long ago at that—although the years go by so frighteningly fast—I barely slept at all during the week before a race!"

The Crank made a sudden pirouette and resumed his tour of the Dauphine. Robert knew what all the activity meant. The garage owner always behaved this way when he was trying to work out something. Like a painter before his subject, he viewed it from all angles before deciding the best course to take.

"Have you agreed to deal with this load of old iron?" Robert asked. "I thought you always refused that kind of job . . ."

All he got from the Crank was a sort of grunt as he went on dancing round the thing.

Then Adèle Bricard looked in and asked if they wanted their coffee. When they were sitting round the kitchen table, the black liquid steaming in the bowls, she jerked her head towards her husband and said to Robert:

"He didn't sleep at all last night. He was jumping about like a fish in a net. I haven't seen him like this since Fangio's first race in France, when he drove for Gordini in the 1948 Grand Prix at Rheims!"

Then she added, for the Crank's benefit:

"I don't know if you are still up to spending sleepless nights like you used to . . ."

"That's enough!" her husband said. "Can't you hold your tongue?"

It seemed to Robert that the pair of them exchanged knowing looks. Without trying to find an explanation, he drank his coffee and got up, saying that he was going to finish off the cylinder head he had started on the previous evening. It was the same every morning. The young mechanic had coffee with the Bricards, then went off to the workshop. The Crank joined him a quarter of an hour later. But on this particular morning Robert had hardly got to his feet, when his employer jumped up and bounced out of the kitchen.

"He really is excited," the boy thought to himself. "I wonder what's cooking." He got down to work. The Crank resumed his stroll round the wreck. After a long pause, he asked suddenly:

"What do you think of this Dauphine?"

The young man did not think much of it. The chassis was certainly buckled; it would have to be straightened on the bench. The front suspension would have to be repaired; the body was pretty badly knocked about . . . Something might be done with the engine, which did not seem to have suffered too badly . . .

"As far as I can see," Robert concluded, "it isn't worth the owner's while to have her repaired. It would cost, at the very least, 3,000 francs . . . Has he made up his mind to have it done?"

"No," said the Crank, screwing up his eyes, "he's selling her for scrap. Not a bad bargain for anyone in the business . . ."

Robert looked hard at his boss, trying to make out what he was getting at. Bricard knew how much money he had got: he could not be thinking of encouraging him to buy that wreck. As it was, it was still worth about a thousand francs, which was a lot more than he had. And there was the cost of putting it right. But the damage had been done. With just a few words, the Crank had dropped the poison in his protégé's ear. Robert looked afresh at the coral Dauphine. She suddenly seemed different.

"Of . . . of course," he stammered, "someone in the trade might be interested. The cost of repairing it wouldn't concern him. Are you interested?"

A mischievous twinkle appeared in the Crank's sky-blue eyes.

"I thought you wanted a car," he said quietly.

Robert felt his eyes prick with tears. Why was Bricard teasing him? He knew he hadn't enough money to start thinking about it!

"It's too much for me," he sighed.

"Something might be arranged."

The boy went red as a tomato, then white as a sheet. He felt as though a steel hand gripped him by the throat.

"How much does the owner want?" he asked in a shaky voice.

"Gave him 1,200. He took it. It wasn't easy. He wouldn't believe that he was making a good deal!"

Robert could have hit the Crank. The swine! He had been playing with him for the last ten minutes. He was calmly telling him that he had bought it for himself!

"As soon as I have a moment," Bricard went on, "I'll see about the licence. You'll have to give me your exact date of birth, I never remember it."

The Crank stopped speaking. You could barely see his eyes, they were so screwed. He shifted awkwardly from one foot to the other.

What was old Bricard talking about? His date of birth? The licence? . . . In *his* name, Robert Daroux's. That must have been what he meant. The boy started to shake all over. He didn't know what to think, he didn't dare . . .

NR 2*

And then the Crank waved his arms in the air and shouted:

"Don't you understand anything, you great ninny? She's yours! She's *your* car!"

He laughed until he sobbed. And the other, the dark, lanky boy, stood gaping at him.

"So you've finally told him!" exclaimed a female voice from the back of the garage.

It was Adèle Bricard who had quietly come in through the far door to be a spectator at the end of the scene.

"That wasn't kind," she went on to her husband. "What did you want to keep him on tenterhooks like that for . . .? Look at the state he's in!"

Robert swallowed painfully and managed to croak: "I can't . . . I haven't . . ."

With a gesture violent enough to decapitate the Venus de Milo, the Crank swept aside his pupil's objections.

"There's no question of money between us! Don't worry about that. We can settle that later! It's a loan, an advance, a present!"

He seized Robert by the shoulder and shouted into his face:

"You'll see! We'll turn her into the most sensational Dauphine, Princess of France and Navarre! She'll make even old Papa Gordini's eyes pop out. I've some ideas, some solutions that . . . Amédée didn't go far enough. Between us we'll show them all what we can do! I've got confidence! I gave you your baptism in engineering! I know you! You've got an eye! The Crank never makes a mistake! And don't you think we'll be content to go off fishing in her on Sunday like a pair of old gentlemen. You'll start with rallies. We'll stay in our class. With one or two improvements, of course! . . . We'll make it hot for the Panhards, the

D K W's, the Austins and the Fiats . . . It's good training! You'll get your hand in! Later on, we'll aim higher . . . You trust old Bricard. I said to you when you were still in short trousers: "You'll race." So it's only the rich who can go in for racing today, is it? Well, we'll see what Robert Daroux, the railwayman's son, can do—!"

Adèle stood with her hands folded across her apron, smiling with delight. Her great big boy of a husband leaped around the workshop, roaring his challenge to the fates. The other big boy, Robert, who was barely out of his teens, echoed his boss's litany.

"It had to happen," she thought to herself. She had felt the approaching crisis for several months. In the evenings she had watched her Auguste going through the racing papers, commenting on the results and cursing the hard times that prevented young men of talent proving themselves on the race track.

"Poor Robert!" he would sometimes exclaim. "I don't know if he'll ever be able to race . . . Do you know what Fangio said to me the other day?"

Adèle did not know what Fangio had said to Auguste, but she could guess. When he had to go to Paris on business, Bricard never failed to go and sniff around the racing departments of the big firms. He always came across one or two of his old friends, drivers or mechanics, whom he had known on the track or in the workshop. Fangio or Chiron or Trintignant had said, or rather repeated, to the old mechanic when he told them about his protégé's ambitions:

"Has he any money? . . . No? . . . Frankly, old son, I don't see a solution. Today, the young driver who wants to break into racing must pay for it. To start with he must get a little sports car. And by that I mean something that can shift—that can do at least a hundred m.p.h. If he's any good—and if he's lucky, because mistakes are costly—he'll make a name for himself. By making a name I don't mean winning, though! I mean just catching a manufacturer's eye. One day, Ferrari, Vanderwel or one of the other big names will say, "Hello, young So-and-so doesn't drive badly. We must try him on one of our cars. The young hopeful will do a couple of laps at the wheel of a Ferrari or a Vanwall. And then he'll find out something: that he has everything to learn. A driver who is unbeatable in his sports car knocking off a hundred m.p.h. will look clumsier than a kid at the wheel of a big racing car. High speed, that is to say over 150 m.p.h., is a world into which only a very few can enter . . . When you think that a car of that sort costs *millions*, and that the tiniest error on the driver's part has every chance of being fatal, you can easily appreciate that before he is tried out by Ferrari, the would-be champion will have spent a fortune!"

"Well then!" Adèle would protest. "How do you think you can give our Robert his chance?"

The Crank would sigh, fit to break a heart of stone. He didn't know. He didn't know any more. In his day the would-be driver had *some* chance, if he was determined enough and had talent enough, of sitting in the driver's seat of a racing car. A humble mechanic might dream of doing so.

"Of course," he would say eventually, "there are the rallies. They are more possible from a financial point of view. The driver who manages to win a prize in one has a chance of getting on to the track, although it's a very slim one! But even when you've got that far, before you can find a manufacturer prepared to subsidize you, you've got to prove yourself in your own car . . . What makes me so mad, you see, Adèle, is that I am sure the boy has it in him. I've seen him from the start. Do you remember? . . . It was when I put him at the wheel of the break down lorry over at the quarries. He instinctively found the right position. Believe me, I can spot them. I don't need to drive with a man for a thousand miles to judge a driver! His position behind the wheel, his natural relaxation are enough for me!"

Adèle would listen. She hoped with all her heart that Robert would eventually reach his long-cherished goal. She had no child and looked on him in a way as her son. She guessed, too, that in some way Robert might be the Crank's revenge against fate. She remembered her Auguste's mad dreams when they were first married: to drive round a track. Bricard had had no chance. The manufacturers for whom he worked had let him try his hand on the most bent-up old crocks. He had even taken part in races. He would certainly have been able to make a career, a minor career, as a racing driver. But the Crank hated mediocrity. He had soon realized that he would never be the equal of a Sommer, a Wimille or a Nuvolari. One Sunday evening he had come in late, with drawn features and a look of utter weariness. He had just taken part in a race at Montlhéry. He had not told Adèle, knowing she was absolutely terrified when she knew he was at the wheel of a racing car.

"That was the last time," he had told her as he sat down before a bowl of steaming soup.

She had looked at him, wide-eyed with astonishment, unable to understand how he could sweep his one ambition clean out of his life with those five words.

"I felt in shape today," he explained. "The car was perfect. Chiron had been really decent. He let me have the best car. There was nothing to stop me winning . . . I came in third—and only just . . ."

The Crank had a lump in his throat and he added, looking Adèle straight in the face:

"No one noticed anything, but I know I'm not up to it. I lack *that*!"

He snapped his fingers. By "that", he meant that spark that makes the champion, that something in the boxer's punch, the sprinter's spurt, the jumper's spring.

"It's better to be a big fish in a little pond. I'd rather be Bugatti's number one mechanic than his number four driver."

Auguste Bricard had never raced again.

Adèle Bricard withdrew discreetly into the back regions. While she went about her household tasks, she heard her husband merrily whistling away, only stopping to discuss the future with Robert.

"Today," Bricard had declared, "our customers will have to lump it. The garage is closed. We're on holiday: we are devoting the entire day to Monsieur Robert Daroux's car!"

Both of them set to work with a will. The great adventure had begun.

❋ ❋ 3 ❋ ❋

AS IT WAS HE who had initiated the great campaign to turn Robert Daroux into a racing driver, the old Crank had taken charge of the proceedings and the young mechanic was naturally second-in-command to his impetuous patron. Towards the end of the first day's work on the wreck of the Dauphine, headquarters received reinforcements in the person of Serge Rivois, the future champion's childhood friend, and Jean Daroux, his younger brother, a schoolboy of sixteen, whose enthusiasm compensated for his lack of technical qualifications. They held a council of war.

A whole corner of the garage had been cleared and set aside for the coral Dauphine. As they dismantled her, they carefully laid out all the parts on a tarpaulin spread out for the purpose. When the wreck had been reduced to a vast quantity of separate components, it looked like a toy "set" for a very young future garage proprietor. This baffling jig-saw puzzle made both Jean and Serge exclaim when they came in:

"Wow!" was Serge's comment on the result of the Crank's and Robert's efforts.

Jean was quite hypnotized by the battered and buckled remains of the bodywork. He made no attempt to disguise his disappointment and cried out:

"Why, it looks like a pile of old tin cans!"

The Crank shrugged disdainfully, but Robert, cut to the quick, nearly lost his temper. His brother might be bright at Latin proses, but he would kindly maintain a respectful silence in the presence of that "pile of old tin cans" in which one day he would be pleased to sit in state.

"All right, keep your shirt on!" Jean said amicably. "It was just a simile! I'm sure you'll make something out of that pile. When you've put the thing together again, if I were you I'd call her Ferblantine,[1] to record how near she was to the scrap heap!"

The Crank started to laugh. It was a good idea: "Ferblantine", sounded well . . .

"Ferblantine . . . Ferblantine," Robert murmured in order to get the feel of the name. "What do you think of it, Serge?" he asked.

The latter was squatting down in front of the "set", carefully examining the different pieces of the puzzle.

He could not care less what name they chose. Ever since Robert had telephoned him at the office of Champigny's little public works department, he had thought of nothing but the Dauphine. His friend had made the briefest mention of the Crank's plans: "We're going to make the car fit to enter sports-car rallies." At once, Serge had started dreaming—dreaming after his own fashion, which was that of a meticulous accountant. The poetry of a column of figures and the symmetry of a balance sheet gave him the same emotions as a symphony. "We are going in for rallies." From among all the various ways in which

[1] *Fer-blanc* is the French for tin, and *ferblantier* for tinker.
—Translator

Robert might one day reach the race track, that of the rallies had obviously been the one they had chosen. If the occasion arose of taking part in this kind of contest, the two friends had agreed to make a team, with Serge concentrating on the navigation and, as it were, the sporting aspects of the business. The meticulous and precise Serge had carefully prepared his role. It must be admitted that, in the hours following his friend's telephone call, Serge neglected his duties a little in order to work away on the little black notebook he might well have entitled, "How to become the perfect rally driver."

As soon as it struck six, he had dashed off to Le Plessis. He had been a hundred yards from the garage when Jean Daroux tapped him on the shoulder. When Robert's younger brother had learned the news from his mother's lips on returning home from school, he had dashed up, too . . .

"Ferblantine?" said Serge. "Why not?"

He was obviously not particularly concerned about the name. He was thinking about something else.

"You'll have to join a club," he announced.

Whereupon, he drew from his pocket his precious black notebook and flipped through the pages.

"What about the Automobile Club of the Ile de France?"

The Crank haughtily ignored these questions of organization. As the rules insisted that each entrant in a rally should be affiliated with a club or a team they would join . . . But for his money all these formalities . . .

"I don't give a damn for all these gentlemen in stiff collars," he said catcgorically. "We don't need them, and we'll race when and where we want."

Jean asked if the badge of the automobile club in question was an attractive one. He was an incurably frivolous boy. The old garage owner protested that he could not care less and they all bickered for a moment. Then Robert pointed out that Ferblantine was in no fit state to receive the humblest of badges and the argument was cut short. But it did not stop everyone going on with his own private daydream. The Crank was lost in mechanical matters . . . Robert saw himself already at the wheel of the little coral car, negotiating the hairpins of a mountain road. Serge, on the other hand, saw himself sitting next to the driver with a pile of cards and notes on his knees, skilfully piloting his friend through a whirling snowstorm. As for Jean, he was at the finish in the front row of the crowd, cheering the winning team, the famous Daroux-Rivois combination!

"I'll see about enrolling tomorrow," said Serge, as unalterable as the right answer to a sum.

They nodded distractedly. Serge consulted his notebook again. He wanted to know what the Crank's plans were. Had he the "standard" or the "special" rating in mind? . . .

When the layman sees cars as different as a Jaguar, an I D Citroën and a Dauphine in the same competition, he is as surprised as he would be to see a race between a zebra, a tortoise and a dragonfly. He does not realize that the organizers work out the results by an index (which means that they multiply the actual time taken by each car by the coefficient accorded to its category). This method enables a Dauphine to beat a Jaguar. By the same token, there is not only a general result but also a result for each category, so that the tortoises, while competing against the zebras and the dragonflies, are also competing among themselves. That is where the distinction between standard and special model comes in. To use the same analogy of the tortoises, these can be divided into two groups: the one running as nature made them, the other having first lightened their shells or eaten some medicinal herb to make them go faster. When it comes to cars, the standard model has been the subject of no special care; whereas the special model has been worked on by specialists.

The decision was an important one.

Which rating would give Robert a chance to make a name for himself?

Serge himself preferred the Standard.

"We'll find ourselves up against ordinary cars," he explained, "but we'll have the advantage of a machine that's perfectly tuned. I have a nasty feeling that the special class might be a bit too crowded . . . What could we do against Dauphines specially designed for racing and driven by champions?"

The result of this speech was to open the floodgates of the Crank's wrath.

"I'm no accountant," he roared. "You may be hot stuff at working out these indices and coefficient thing-ama jigs, but what I say is this: the standard rating's fine for little minor competitions, but what Robert needs is to make a splash. What use is it to us if he wins the Romorantin Rally? That isn't the way to get to drive a Ferrari! But if he carries off the Liège-Rome-Liège, then the big manufacturers will consider him. Between us we'll tune a car that will knock spots off every other special in the world!"

Serge gave way with good grace. He had no intention of starting a controversy. He just wanted the matter to be thrashed out . . . As the team's organizer he wanted to know where he stood.

Passions, suddenly aroused, died down again. They returned to practical and more immediate matters. Several times during the day, Robert had returned to his main worry: his lack of funds. And each time the

Crank had begged him not to think about it. He had paid Gavard. Everything was settled there. As for the repairs, they'd come to some arrangement.

"You'll need what money you've got," the garage owner had told him, "for the insurance. Don't forget that if you go in for competitions, you require special insurance . . . As for the other expenses, we'll do things as cheaply as we can. We'll beat out the panels at Saumer's place. He's a good pal of mine who has a place over at Vitry. He's got the equipment. We'll pick up the spare parts cheaply enough from the local traders. People in the trade always help each other.

In spite of these assurances, Robert was tormented by the money problem. He made use of the presence of Serge and Jean to bring it up again. The Crank tried to shut him up but he was adamant.

"I mean it, Monsieur Bricard, things must be cut and dried."

"How obstinate can you get!" groaned the garage owner. "I told you I was giving you the wreck as a present."

"But what about the rest?" cried Robert, who was scruple incarnate. "How shall I pay for that?"

"I've saved up nearly 500 francs," said Serge. "It's all yours. We're teaming up so it's only fair I pay my share of the expenses."

Jean Daroux didn't want to be left out. He had a superb record player and a record collection he was proud of. He offered to sell the lot to help his brother.

"You know," he added, "that I've got some stuff you simply can't find today: vintage Benny Goodmans and Louis Armstrongs . . . they'll fetch quite a bit!"

"What's this?" asked the Crank, whose musical tastes were those of the early 1900s.

"Jazz men!" Jean explained. "People collect their early recordings . . . I've got quite a few. And together with the record player, I'm bound to get nearly a thousand francs."

"You're a good lad," Bricard said, "but you mustn't sacrifice your treasure . . . I'll make a deal with you. Your records and record player will be a sort of guarantee . . . If Robert finds himself unable to repay me the cost of the repairs, you'll sell them to pay his debts . . ."

"That seems fair to me," said Serge—the accountant. "Tomorrow I'll bring you the 500 francs for the preliminary expenses . . ."

This cataract of sacrifices and generosity might have gone on for a good deal longer had not an enormous American car drawn up outside the Garage de l'Avenir . . . The Crank and the three youngsters were awed into silence. The Rue Bon-Repos had never seen its like. Long and low and silvery grey, it looked like a magazine illustrator's idea of a flying saucer. An elegantly dressed gentlemen emerged from it and entered the garage.

"I should like to speak to Monsieur Auguste Bricard," he said.

The Crank stepped forward. Yes, he was Bricard. What was it about?

"I am Gaston Mercier of the Garage du Soleil near the Gare de Lyon."

The Crank nodded without speaking. His eyes narrowed as he examined this large expensive-looking gentleman with tanned face and an English tweed suit of impeccable cut. He automatically took the hand offered him. Poor Monsieur Bricard, he felt like the owner of a flea circus being greeted as a fellow impresario by Messrs. Barnum and Bailey.

Hiding his astonishment, he managed to articulate: "What can I do for you?"

Gaston Mercier's glance travelled over all the junk

that cluttered up the barn. For a couple of seconds his eyes rested on the coral Dauphine laid out in its separate components on the tarpaulin, hesitated on the three young people standing behind the Crank, then returned to the latter. With exquisite politeness he said:

"I should be awfully grateful if I could have a minute with you . . ."

Bricard passed a damp hand over his balding skull. He was in a dilemma. He felt he could not decently take his visitor into what he called his office, that ghastly wooden hutch where he could not even stand upright himself. Robert came to his aid.

"We've an errand to do, Monsieur Bricard," he said. "We'll be back in a quarter of an hour."

Robert went out, taking his brother and Serge with him.

"This is why I have come to see you," Mercier began, as soon as they were out of earshot. "Monsieur Gavard is one of my regular customers . . . He came to my office this afternoon and told me about yesterday's accident. He also told me that he had sold you his car for the scrap price . . ."

The elegant Paris garage proprietor smiled and added in soft, almost caressing tones: "I scolded him."

"Oh yes," said the Crank.

"Monsieur Gavard is a good friend of mine," Monsieur Mercier went on. "He has helped me on several occasions. I immediately thought that this accident would provide me with the opportunity to pay him back. I've been looking for an opportunity to do him a good turn and I think I've found the way. That is why I'm here. I've come for the wreck. I'm prepared to buy it back. I know you gave Gavard a very fair price. I will give you a hundred francs above that, as I see you have already taken it to pieces. That will pay for your work . . ."

Up to that point the Crank had been listening rather uncomfortably to Mercier. He was ill at ease with this smooth character. But as soon as the other said what had brought him, Bricard relaxed at once He felt he was back in his depth. It was to do with a car, so he did have something in common with this dandified garage man.

"I can't do it," he said simply. "She's not mine any more. I've given her to Robert, my mechanic . . ."

"I'm sure we can arrange something," Mercier insisted. "Perhaps the young man would like to sell the car?"

"No, he plans to reassemble her. As you see, we've started work already . . . I'm giving him a hand."

Monsieur Mercier's handsome bronzed face darkened. He was visibly very put out. He understood, of course, that a tiny profit of a hundred francs wouldn't tempt the boy . . . But he was really set on helping his friend Gavard. Surely something could be arranged, seeking they were both in the trade . . .?

The Crank knitted his brows in thought. This Parisian chap was really a very obliging sort of friend, he would have liked to help him, one should be able to help a fellow motor engineer . . . But, as sure as his name was Bricard, he could not see the answer to the problem; Robert would never find another car at such a price.

"Yes—yes, I understand," Monsieur Mercier murmured. "But all the same, don't you think he might part with it if I were to make him a—er—shall we say, a more substantial offer? I would be prepared to go up to 500 francs . . ."

The Crank could not conceal his amazement. His fellow garage owner had an odd way of doing business.

Admittedly, he wanted to help Gavard, but—1,700 francs for the wreck! How much would he give Gavard for it then?

Mercier hesitated for barely a second, then said:

"I gave him to understand he could get nearly 1,800 francs for his car . . ."

The old mechanic exploded:

"If I'm not mistaken," he exclaimed, "you made me appear a crook to this gentleman. He thinks I have swindled him of 600 francs."

The Paris garage owner tried to calm Bricard.

"Don't get upset," he began, "Gavard doesn't think you're a crook."

"That's what you say: he isn't here to contradict you! . . . Listen, Monsieur Mercier, I'll give you a piece of advice. You know perfectly well that the 1,200 francs I gave your client is the maximum he could normally expect to get for his wreck. So I didn't treat him unfairly. If you want to give him a present, that's your business. As things stand, it would seem simpler to me if you were just to give him the sum of 600 francs which constitutes the difference between the actual value of the car and what you have offered him for it. After all, it's your money . . ."

Mercier listened to the Crank's lecture with tightened lips. The owner of the silver-grey flying saucer was plainly not very pleased!

"I am sorry," he said coldly, "but I do not require your advice. I stand by my offer, which is 1,700 francs for the Dauphine."

"I'm not selling her," snapped Bricard.

"Does the car belong to you or to your mechanic?"

The Crank had reached the end of his tether. His face was red, his pale eyes shot murderous glances and he was trembling with rage. He flung up his arms and pointing to Robert and his companions, said:

"Ask him yourself!"

After tactfully staying at a distance, they were beginning to drift back, thinking the conversation was over.

"Robert!" Bricard roared. "This gentleman, after telling people I'm a crook, wants to buy your car. He's offering 1,700 francs for it!"

The young mechanic stopped dead on the threshold, thunderstruck. He had never seen his master in such a state . . .

"S-seventeen hundred francs?" he stammered.

He looked uncertainly first at the Crank, then at Mercier and finally at Serge and his brother. It seemed a vast sum to him, but he could not understand why his boss was asking what he thought. He still did not consider himself as the wreck's rightful owner. In any case, it was up to the Crank to decide, if it was a good offer.

"Well?" the garage owner said sharply.

"You'd make a handsome profit," murmured Mercier hopefully. "It's up to Monsieur Bricard to decide," Robert murmured.

Monsieur Bricard stamped his foot.

"I'm asking *your* opinion!" he shouted.

"I—er—well—I'd rather keep the car," the mechanic admitted.

The Crank, suddenly calm again, turned with an Olympian air to Mercier and said:

"Do you hear that? That's settled then." And he added, "If you take the first street to the right and follow it all the way, you'll come out onto the main Paris road."

"Very well," the Parisian murmured. "I'll remember how you received me, when the time comes . . ."

Swinging round on his heel, he returned to his car. the expensive limousine moved silently away.

"What's been going on?" asked Serge, the first to recover from the bewilderment that had seized the three young people.

"Huh!" exclaimed the Crank with superb contempt. "Absolutely nothing! That character's a little over-generous with his presents and reputations. The one he gave me was not to my liking, so I showed him the door. One good turn, as they say!"

❋ ❋ 4 ❋ ❋

TWO DAYS HAD GONE BY. After the feverish excitement of the first few hours, Robert's and the Crank's passion for the coral Dauphine had, as it were, settled down to its cruising speed. A long day's work had been necessary to transform the wreck into a pile of separate pieces; it would take at least a month to put those pieces together to make what would be virtually a new car. There was no question of the two mechanics of the Garage de l'Avenir, boss and employer, spending the whole of their time on the future racing car. It wasn't that they did not want to,but they had to think of their customers, too. It had therefore been decided that during business hours they would behave as if the Dauphine was still stuck in the pond at that crossroad. But as soon as it struck six, farewell to their dreary mercenary tasts: they grappled with Ferblantine until it was past eight o'clock. Adèle Bricard had to use all her authority to make the two men abandon their toy. The Crank had tyrannically refused to allow Robert to come back to the garage after dinner.

"I don't want you to kill yourself working on her," he said, very reasonably. "You've been waiting for this car for years. So be patient! Anyway, you won't last out, if you spend every night on her. You can work two hours a day on Ferblantine plus Saturday afternoon and Sunday morning. You have got to have a complete rest on Sunday afternoon. You mustn't get besotted!"

Robert had agreed. These good resolutions had been taken after the departure of Gaston Mercier, sent on his way so happily by Bricard. As soon as Robert, Serge and Jean had gone, the Crank had a hurried supper . . . and returned to Ferblantine. The mechanic had not failed to notice, the next morning, that his boss had put in some overtime. He had remarked on it. The Crank's only reply had been to mutter that he always found it hard to get to sleep and that he found it relaxing to tinker with something.

Robert Daroux, forbidden to stay on at the Garage de l'Avenir after 8 p.m., champed at the bit for hours before he got off to sleep. And to make matters worse, all mention of Ferblantine was taboo at the family table. The fact was that Monsieur and Madame Daroux had not greeted the news of their son's acquisition of the wreck with much enthusiasm. Cars are expensive things . . . Robert and Jean had tried to explain in detail how it was that repairing Ferblantine would actually cost them fantastically little. Under an avalanche of technical arguments, the parents had given up. They knew that the moment had come, that moment they had dreaded ever since the day their eldest son had announced that he was going to be a racing driver. Madame Daroux, especially, had never become resigned to the idea.

"Enough people kill themselves on the roads," she would sometimes sigh. "And you want to race! I would never feel at ease if you had a car!"

As for Monsieur Daroux, he spent a sleepless night

every time the paper announced the death of a racing champion . . .

Father and mother had been silent. But Robert and Jean had seen their expressions grow a little more anxious than usual. They tacitly stopped talking of Ferblantine and their plans.

Robert could not talk about his car over the evening meal, or even afterwards alone with his brother Jean, for the latter was hard at work preparing for his *baccalauréat* exam. The young mechanic was therefore left alone with his thoughts . . . But he was no idle dreamer. He knew that before he could hope one day to win a rally, he would have to do a lot of work and suffer many disappointments. For the moment, his number one problem was—as the team had decided to enter Ferblantine in the special class—to study all the possible modifications that would turn the Dauphine into an unbeatable racer. The Crank had his own ideas. "But he hasn't forbidden me to work out better ones myself," thought Robert. So he took out his drawing board (little used since he got his mechanic's certificate), his books and all the mass of information he had been collecting on the subject.

Monsieur Gaston Mercier had come to the garane on Tuesday. It was on Friday, towards half past nine in the evening, that the young mechanic raised his head from his drawing board. On the other side of the table, Jean was struggling with a mathematics problem.

"I think I'm on to something," the elder boy said thoughtfully. "We should modify the cam-shaft."

He handed his brother the sheet of drawing paper on which he had sketched the thing. Jean glanced at it briefly so as not to disappoint Robert, but in point of fact he was in the same position as an Egyptologist faced with hieroglyphics in the days before Champollion's discovery of the Rosetta Stone. His brother's copious explanations made things no clearer. Jean just had no head for mechanics.

"You ought to go and talk about it to the Crank," he said. "He must still be messing about with Ferblantine, the selfish old devil . . . I'll go with you if you like . . . I've had enough of this miserable work for tonight."

Robert did not need to be asked twice. He had been longing to go to the garage but had not dared break the rule. If he went along with Jean, just for the walk, it would be different. Besides, he wasn't going to get down to work, only to discuss . . .

It was a lovely May night. The two young people strolled along in a leisurely fashion towards the Rue Bon-Repos. When they were fifty yards from the garage, they noticed that there was no light on in the workshop but only in the kitchen of the little house tacked on to one side of the old barn.

"The Crank isn't there," said Robert in a disappointed voice.

"That's odd," observed his brother, "Madame Bricard told me yesterday that he had gone quite crazy over that car and never left the workshop before midnight. Come on! He may not have gone far . . ."

They went nearer. The double door of the garage was half open. The inside was plunged in darkness. The two boys thought they heard a slight sound.

"Monsieur Bricard!" Jean called softly.

"He's not there," objected Robert. "What would he be doing in the pitch dark?"

"But you heard it, too," protested Jean. "It was like someone knocking into a sheet of metal . . . Perhaps the fuses have blown . . . and he has stumbled and hurt himself."

It was a plausible suggestion. Besides, it was strange that Bricard had not shut the door to the street. The light switch was at the far end of the barn, near the little door that led to the garden.

"I'll go," Robert said. "You stay here. Otherwise you'll be floundering around in all this mess."

Robert disappeared into the darkness. He had no need of a light, knowing from long experience exactly where to find each obstacle. He passed close by the workbenches ranged against the left-hand wall, taking care not to stray from them and bang into two engines resting on trestles to his right . . . Beyond the benches there was a drill set up and farther on a lathe running parallel with the wall. One . . . two . . . three paces. Look out! Robert was suddenly aware of a dark mass between himself and the door. He remembered how that afternoon he had put the two front seats and the back seat from Ferblantine there. The Crank himself had told him he ought to put them somewhere else. He carefully walked round the black shape. His eyes had now become accustomed to the dark and were just able to see things.

"Well?" Jean said from the doorway. "Have you found the switch?"

It seemed to Robert that something was moving two paces away from him, near the door and between Rosalie, Bricard's old car, and the wall. He shivered.

"What's got into me?" he wondered. "Am I scared of something?"

He stared into the space between the car and the wall, a hole in the darkness that filled the barn. This time he could not see a thing.

He mechanically turned towards his brother to tell him not to worry—that he was going to put on the light . . . He had just opened his mouth to speak when . . . he felt a dull blow on his chest! The pain made him cry out . . . Doubled up, he staggered back, staring in front of him . . . In a sort of haze he thought he saw the little door to the garden open. A gust of cold air caught him in the face. He stumbled against one of the engines and fell over backwards. Jean called out:

"What's going on? Have you hurt yourself?"

Robert got up painfully. He heard himself moan as though in a dream.

"It's nothing, I must have bumped into something . . ."

Stretching out both hands in front of him, like a blind man, he once more advanced towards the switch. The draught was making the little door bang. He could see through it a sliver of sky, a satiny blue pricked with stars. His right hand reached the switch and light flooded the barn.

He turned round and gave an exclamation.

The Crank was lying on the ground three yards away from him, near Rosalie's bonnet. He seemed to be peacefully asleep, with his arms stretched straight by his sides and his head resting easily on the ground.

"Oh n-no!" stammered Jean, who had just rejoined his brother.

The two boys, unable to take their eyes off the motionless figure, held their breath, not daring to make a gesture, as though they wanted to stop the inexorable march of time.

"He's dead!" sobbed Robert.

The spell was broken. He had to go on living, to look properly at the recumbent figure and bear his responsibility.

He knelt down beside the Crank and felt his pulse: his face cleared.

"Quick!" he said, straightening up. "His heart is beating! We must tell Adèle and ring a doctor. Quickly!"

The sequence of events was like a nightmare. Adèle

started screaming like a siren. The local doctors were all out. One from Champigny said he'd come as soon as possible. When he got there, he found the Rue de Bon-Repos in an uproar. There were nearly fifty people clustering round the garage and the cottage. A policeman, whom no one had sent for but who happened to be passing, had decided to take over the investigations. He was arguing with people who had seen nothing but whose sole ambition *was* to see something. The doctor managed to elbow his way into the barn where the onlookers, crowded together like travellers on the Métro in the rush hour, surrounded Madame Bricard, Robert and Jean Daroux and a man sitting on the ground holding his head and yelling that he'd die of asphyxiation if they didn't give him some air.

The Crank was not dead. He had just been well and truly bashed—on the back of the neck with an adjustable wrench.

They carried him to his bedroom, where the doctor examined him. Two inspectors from the police station, who had been called by the witnesses, took down his statement. They were able to disentangle from his curses the facts that he had lingered to watch television after dinner and, as he had been bored by the show, had decided about 9:35 p.m. to "have a look round" the workshop; that he had opened the little door and had been about to put on the light when an H-bomb had exploded inside his head . . .

It did not need a Sherlock Holmes to guess that his attacker, who had broken open the main door leading to the street, had been surprised by the garage owner and had hit him in order to make his get-away. He had been about to leave when the arrival of Robert and Jean Daroux had forced him to hide . . . and to strike again. This time he had decamped without further ado and had doubtless been swallowed up by the garden.

"It was definitely a prowler," one of the inspectors concluded. "Has he taken anything?"

The Crank did not know. All he was worrying about at the moment was his (literal) pain in the neck. Jean and Robert went off to the garage with an inspector on each side of them. As far as they could see, nothing had been touched. The most valuable tools, such as the micrometer calipers and the caliper-squares, were in their places . . . Robert was ferreting round the barn when he suddenly came to a halt in front of Ferblantine's seats. One of the front ones was missing!

"It can't be!" exclaimed the inspector. "You must have moved it without thinking! Take a look!"

After five minutes, they had to accept the evidence: the seat had completely disappeared!

"When our villain was surprised, he must have snatched up the first thing he found in the dark," said the other inspector. "It's peculiar, but you come across some queer things in our job!"

Robert could not understand it. In any case he was not particularly interested: at that moment all he was worrying about was the Crank's condition.

"It's queer, all right," Jean agreed. "But I'm sure that when you've caught him, Monsieur Bricard's attacker will give us an explanation of such a fantastic theft . . . There's a logical explanation for everything."

Jean was obviously ready to go into the philosophy class.

❋ ❋ 5 ❋ ❋

NATURE HAS GIVEN MAN only one head and two arms. However efficient this equipment may be, it cannot cope with every situation. Robert Daroux discovered this fact on the third day after the Master of the Garage de l'Avenir had been immobilized.

As the Crank had a skull as tough as a piston, he had triumphantly survived the blow with the adjustable spanner that his attacker had crashed down on the nape of his neck. After examination and auscultation and X-rays, they found that head, so full of ambitious plans, was quite intact. Nevertheless, the doctors had been definite: "Absolutely no work for two weeks; complete rest and quiet and lots of nourishing food."

The Crank had received the recommendations of the Faculty of Medicine with shouts of rage and threats to sabotage, for the rest of his life, all those cars which bear the insignia of the doctor driver. It was then that Adèle Bricard had gone into action. She was normally a gentle, self-effacing little woman, but when the occasion called for it she could prove even more of a tyrant than her spouse.

"Auguste," she said calmly, "you will be silent. You will do as the gentlemen say."

The gentlemen in question were the doctors of the clinic where, on the day after his attack, the Crank had a thorough examination. The garage owner obeyed, but when he got back to Plessis he went straight into the workshop and seemed determined to stay there.

"Those sawbones don't know a thing!" he pontificated. "I feel perfectly all right and Robert can't manage by himself. There's too much work!"

Suiting his action to his words, the herculean Auguste Bricard seized a great hunk of metal with his powerful hands.

"A-ha!" he grunted.

And an indescribable expression of stupefaction spread over his childlike countenance.

The Hercules found himself sitting on the dusty floor; the hunk of metal had not moved an inch.

"If you play the fool like that again," Adèle remarked mildly, "it will be two months you have to spend in bed."

The Crank did not try again. Although he tried to pass it off, he was pretty scared. He had never had a day's illness in his life. The first sign of weakness in a constitution that he had always taken for granted really frightened him.

"It's true I was shaken up a bit . . ." he said.

"You go and lie down," was the inflexible Adèle's gentle advice.

"But Robert . . ."

The young mechanic intervened. Monsieur Bricard was not to worry, the garage would carry on without him. He would do all the work in double-quick time. Ferblantine could wait. They'd get on with her later.

"You won't be able to do it," groaned the Crank.

"He'll do what he can," Adèle said. "And you can go to bed and just pray everything goes right until you can put your finger into the pie again."

"If you *don't*," she added, with a meaning look at the poor chap who was weakly leaning on the workbench for support, "you know what to expect . . ."

The Crank trotted off dutifully in the direction of the house. He was tamed.

Robert had said he would do the work in double-quick time. He kept his word, or rather he tried, for no one can do the impossible. It was the month of May and a lot of customers, looking ahead to the holiday rush, were bringing in their cars for overhaul. They would drive up to the garage, thinking that a quick look at the ignition and the brakes would be all that was needed. Their faces fell when a conscientious Robert told them that as well as "a quick look" they would have to consider having their valves ground in or the clutch plate replaced.

The work piled up. It was all very well Robert redoubling his efforts. It was on the third day of working like a galley slave that he had to admit two arms and one head are sometimes insufficient. Particularly the head, as it has only two eyes.

It was three in the afternoon when a Simca Montlhéry Aronde stopped in front of the Garage de l'Avenir. The driver came in and asked to see the boss. He was an ordinary sort of man with nothing particular to remember him by—vaguely sporty looking. As the boss was out, he said straight out what had brought him. He was keen on rallies and a friend had mentioned Auguste Bricard to him. The friend had himself heard of Monsieur Bricard from a motor-racing enthusiast who owned an M.G. and was a customer of the Garage de l'Avenir. Attracted by the Crank's reputation, he wanted him to look after his car . . .

Robert managed to dam this flood of words and inform the man that the Crank was in bed as the result of an accident.

"Come back in two weeks; the boss will be on the job again by then!"

"Er . . .well . . ."

The man scratched his head doubtfully. He'd have liked to get fixed up . . . He had a little sketch on him . . . Even if he were in bed, Bricard could have a look at it and give him an estimate.

"All right!" Robert said, annoyed at the waste of his time and aware that the only way to get rid of the fellow was to give him some sort of satisfaction. "Give me your piece of paper. He'll say when you can come back . . ."

Leaving the rally enthusiast there, he went into the cottage. He was crossing the garden when Adèle Bricard came out to meet him. The Crank was asleep. He wasn't to be disturbed, his wife was quite definite about that.

"That's a nuisance," Robert said. "This chap's very insistent. He might be a good customer."

Adèle took the sketch.

"Don't worry. I'll deal with it."

They both went back to the garage together. Through the open door to the street, Robert could see the Aronde, but there was no sign of the man.

"What a curious character," Robert thought. "Where can he have got to . . .?"

At that moment, a metallic sound made him turn round. The visitor had not gone. He had made his way into the heap of old junk at the far end of the garage. Surrounded by discarded wings, he looked at the young man and Madame Bricard in embarrassment at being caught.

"I'm f-frightfully sorry," he said, "I can't resist bric-à-brac. I'm afraid I . . ."

"There's no lack of it here," answered Robert, who was made uneasy by the other's ridiculous situation.

The man clumsily struggled out of the heap of battered metal; there was a sinister tearing sound. He had just caught his trousers on something.

"My husband is resting," Adele said coldly. "Come back in two weeks if you want to see him."

She handed him his sketch. He took it, stammered his apologies and scuttled off to his car.

"There's a queer one," commented Madame Bricard when the over-curious visitor had disappeared at the wheel of his Aronde. "He has very peculiar manners."

She thought a moment before she went on:

"It can't go on like this. You've too much to do, the customers are all complaining . . ."

"Don't worry," Robert protested. "There is a little delay at the moment, but I'll catch up . . ."

"No. Besides I don't want you to skimp on the job. You see you can't do it all by yourself. You can't even turn your back for a moment . . . Suppose we had a thief here. He could very well disappear with something . . ."

Robert was bound to admit that it wasn't easy. He could not leave the job.

"We must find someone," Adèle decided. "Auguste will know the sort of man we need."

"I need only stamp my foot, to bring forth legions," the Roman general used to say. Madame Bricard might almost have classed herself his equal without undue boasting, for she did not even have to tap her foot on the bare earth floor of the barn. The next day, just before noon, a sort of marmoset appeared at the garage. Jules Langlois did look just like a marmoset dressed up as a man. He was small, wizened and as agile as a monkey. A check cloth cap stuck on one side of his head gave his face a foxy look, which was accentuated by a pair of sharp prying eyes. He had the accent and cheeky wit of the real *titi*—the Parisian version of the London cockney.

"Afternoon!" he said, raising a finger to his unspeakable headgear. "Who might you be?"

Robert gazed at this comic little creature and answered that he was the mechanic.

"I'm looking for a job . . . You got anything for me?"

This mechanical monkey was a gift from heaven. Robert called Adèle Bricard. She asked the applicant all the usual questions. Without being suspicious, she liked to know the sort of people she dealt with, and Jules Langlois belonged to that category of individuals classed as "unstable". To judge from his explanations and the bundle of grubby paper she produced, he could not bear to stay more than two months in the same place. As he had been in most of the Paris garages, he explained his decision to try the suburbs. Having had a series of set-to's with his landlord, whom he seemed to have it in for in no uncertain terms, he had taken a room in a Champigny hotel "just by the river, real countrified . . . I'll be able to go fishing just like that, see!" As chance had brought him to the district, he was looking for a job near his new domicile.

Adèle did not mind Jules Langlois . . . You don't need social airs and graces to be able to repair an engine. In any case it would only be a matter of taking him on for a few weeks . . . He was led to the Crank's bedside. The latter had received a severe talking-to from his wife the previous evening. When he learned that she was thinking of bringing a stranger into the workshop, he had first of all raved and shouted. But when Adèle had heavily stressed the untoward demands that were being made on Robert, he piped down. He was extremely fond of the young man, and Adèle had said, "He won't stand up to it. I'm sure he's lost weight since he has been on his own."

Auguste Bricard had therefore grumblingly agreed in principle to their taking on a mechanic. Still, there is quite a step from principle to practice. The Crank made a face when he saw his future employee. Jules had to give his references all over again. His previous employers were unanimous in praise of his efficiency . . .

"When do you want to start?" asked the garage owner.

"This afternoon, if that suits you."

So it was that within three days the Garage de l'Avenir (temporarily) lost its boss and (again, temporily) acquired a new hand.

There was no doubt that Jules was an excellent mechanic. Nor that he was an incorrigible chatterbox. Robert was, without being taciturn, on the reserved side, but the marmoset possessed the art of finding the subject to make the most clam-like people open up. Within a day of his arrival, he knew all about Ferblantine. The day after, the future champion Robert Daroux had no warmer supporter.

"You take my word for it, kid," he said, "the boss is right. If you want to make 'em sit up and take notice, you start with the rallies. Win your first victory and the manufacturers will be all round you. No more money worries: a works car, wages and expenses . . . Now I'm here, you can get back to work on Ferblantine after six o'clock!"

As the garage could now operate normally, there was indeed no reason why Robert should not start on his own car again. The Crank himself loudly encouraged him to do so. Besides, in two or three days, he would be up and about again with the doctor's blessing. There was no question of his doing his normal amount of work, but he could potter about for an hour or two and keep his mind and hands occupied without straining himself. It would be excellent for his morale. After a week of high drama, life was returning to its normal course. They had almost forgotten the Crank's attacker, for whom the police were still making—they said—an intensive search . . . Imperceptibly, everything became as it was before, except that they had Jules. For the mechanic, fired with enthusiasm for the little team's grandiose plans, had quickly joined in their activity. He voluntarily put in two hours a day on Ferblantine.

"Where have you put the radiator?" he asked Robert one evening. "There is a sort of mark on the motor unit. I have a feeling it may have damaged it a little in the crash . . ."

The whole team was assembled. Jean Daroux, perched on one of the benches, dominated the scene, but only because he did not know what else to do. Serge Rivois had taken off his jacket and put on dungarees over his city suit. He was squatting down cleaning parts in a basin filled with paraffin.

The Crank, sitting on a chair with his head tied up in a white bandage that made him look like a bogus fakir, supervised operations, in the intervals of fighting cunningly with Adèle, who kept begging him to go to bed. It was his first day out.

Robert hunted for the radiator Jules had asked for. In the end he found it under the lathe.

"You'll lose something in the end," the marmoset teased him. "Yesterday I was looking for the back seat to measure the body, but I couldn't find it."

The Crank could not prevent himself exclaiming indignantly:

"I've no criticism of your work, but all the same, when I hear a mechanic talk of measuring a body with a seat!"

A persistent Jules explained that he "just wanted a rough estimate".

Robert started to laugh.

"Don't worry," he said, "since the attack, Monsieur Bricard sees red when you mention anything to do with upholstery. As for the back seat and the front one the thief spared, I'll have to bring them down. They're in my room. I didn't know where to put them, and Jean and I use them as armchairs."

Adèle Bricard came in. This time it was final. The Crank had to go back to his room.

"Anyway, it is eight o'clock," she went on. "You've all worked quite enough. I'm sending you all home. That way I'll get hold of Auguste!"

Everyone reluctantly stopped what he was doing. The first to go was Jules. "Champigny's quite a way," he said.

The three young people were about to take their leave of the Bricards, after Adèle had twice again called them to order, when Monsieur Médor appeared, or, to be precise, the dog called Médor and the gentleman he dragged along on the end of his leash.

Monsieur Médor was the proprietor of a little café at the end of the Rue Bon-Repos, some fifty yards from the garage. Unlike any ordinary self-respecting café keeper, he had omitted—either out of negligence or out of snobbery—giving his establishment a name. For convenience sake and because it was easier to say than "Monsieur Caramantoucy", his rightful name, he was known by the name of his beloved dog, a shaggy Briard sheepdog called Médor. At the same time every evening, Médor and Monsieur would take their little constitutional.

The group greeted Monsieur Médor, who answered with a number of civil but somewhat involved remarks concerning the mildness of this particular May. The Crank was invited to say how he felt . . .

"A little bird tells me," the café keeper said with an air of importance, "that it will not be long before we have news of your assailant. There is something in the wind . . ."

The garage owner, Madame and the young ones stared, round-eyed, at the man with the dog.

Monsieur Médor looked round him conspiratorially and said in confidential tones:

"For two days there has been a man spending almost his entire time in my establishment . . . Some sort of representative, he says, but I myself think he's a detective. I can smell them, you know!"

"Really?" said the Crank.

He did not like Monsieur Médor and a terrible headache was hammering at his temples. He was now longing to get to bed.

Monsieur Médor once more peered up and down the street.

It was still as deserted as before. He whispered:

"While we were talking, the business of you being attacked cropped up . . . He asked me all kinds of questions . . ."

"People love a bit of gossip," Adèle put in.

"Yes, of course, people must chatter," sighed the café keeper. "But there was something else . . . I'm sure that this man settled on my place in order to watch the street . . ."

The Crank's headache was really too bad. He muttered a vague goodnight and went off with Madame. Monsieur Médor, disappointed at the lack of success he had had with his story, resumed his walk, still towed by the dog.

"Do you believe his story?" Robert asked his brother when they got home.

"Bah!" said Jean. "He's got precious little work to do, that chap: he must have something to keep him occupied . . . I expect he reads detective stories . . ."

"That's what I think."

"All the same," Jean went on, "I don't know, but it seems to me that since Ferblantine arrived at the Garage de l'Avenir, there have been some funny goings-on in the Rue Bon-Repos."

Robert shrugged his shoulders.

"You read too many thrillers yourself," he grumbled.

Jean protested. Hc was boning up on his mathematics: he had no time to waste.

The young mechanic did not answer. Although he didn't want to admit it, what his younger brother had said made him think. It coincided with a vague idea he had not dared put into words. It was true that in the past week some peculiar things had been going on round the garage . . .

6

EXTRACTS FROM THE LOG of Ferblantine, kept by the meticulous Serge Rivois.

May 18th

Things are moving fast. Ferblantine will soon be a reality. The Crank is all right now. He still wears a little round of adhesive tape like a piece of pink confetti on the back of his head, but the doctor has allowed him to go back to work. Jules Langlois, the mechanic Madame Bricard hired, asked if he should look for another job, but the Crank said he would like him to stay on at the garage . . . "As I have started to take my holidays," he said, "I'm going to continue them until after the 'Twenty-four Hours' at Le Mans. I want to get on with Ferblantine." Jules seemed pleased enough not to leave the Rue Bon-Repos . . . That chap has not done anything to me personally, but I can't get to like him. Robert says he is very nice and that his cynical manner hides a heart of gold. Personally, I think he is a phony. The other day I happened to go into a *café-tabac* in Champigny and saw Jules standing in line at the betting window with a roll of money in his hand. . .[1]

[1] Bets may be placed on horse races in France at many cigar stores.

So he does bet on horses, even though he said yesterday, so that the Crank could hear, that "the nags turned him up, he'd rather have brake horsepower". He knows Bricard hates gamblers and wanted to butter him up. I don't like that sort of character.

May 20th

A great day for Ferblantine yesterday. The Crank decided to spend the day visiting the scrap yards to try and get cheap replacements for the condemned parts of the car. I didn't want to miss a party like that so I asked the office for the day off. We left at three, the Crank, Robert and I, in Rosalie. Robert was driving. Jean couldn't come. He had classes and, anyway, his exam's getting close. That kid really is cramming; we barely ever see him . . .

We started our grand tour with the motor graveyards off the N. 4. The Crank knows them all . . . He made a sort of royal progress round them. I had no idea he was as well known as that. He's a real celebrity in his own world and we never realized it.

Besides, all the scrap dealers wanted to know the circumstances of the attack on him; they had read about it in the papers. They were astonished when they learned that the villain had fled with one of the Dauphine's front seats. The reporters had left that part out . . . Of course they covered the incident in only a few lines, and a seat isn't important. Figus, a scrap dealer at Tournan dragged us off into his yard when he heard about the theft. He had just picked up a coral Dauphine, identical with Ferblantine. It lacked the rear half. It was the result of a skid on a wet road, said Figus, a cheerful fat fellow. The ghastly accidents that furnished him with his stock in trade did not appear to have damped his spirits!

The front seats of the wreck were new; they had not

a mark on them. Figus had them out in the twinkling of an eye.

"Take them," he said to the Crank.

The latter asked how much he owed. Figus looked most offended. Why, nothing of course. Had the Crank forgotten the good turn he had done him ten years ago? It was his, Figus', way of settling a small part of his debt. And what was more, Robert could ferret round the yard and take anything that was of any use to him.

By noon, we found ourselves at Le Plessis-Chenet, at the beginning of the Southern Motorway. We had lunch in a restaurant. The Crank was in terrific form; so was Robert. We had got some stupendous things: the seats—Figus had insisted on giving us both, a camshaft, three shock absorbers, a complete windscreen wiper with its motor in perfect condition, and numerous other parts. As we stowed away our finds in Rosalie, I made a note in my notebook of how much we had paid for each. The morning had really been fabulous: we had spent barely twenty francs and that only because the Crank had insisted on buying the windscreen wiper from the dealer who had given it to us.

"There are some people I don't like accepting presents from," our mentor had said when we had left him.

The afternoon was no less successful. At Orly we picked up the four-speed gearbox Ferblantine needed. We had been beginning to despair of finding one when in a huge junk yard Robert spotted a Dauphine Gordini, reduced to its basic principles. We got the box at a very reasonable price. It only needs a pinion changing. Good business and a good day!

May 23rd

This evening, after six o'clock, we went to Saumer—the body repairer at Vitry to whom the Crank has given the job of restoring Ferblantine to her original shape. Robert and he had taken Saumer the body of the wreck two days beforehand. They wanted to find out how the work was going. I went with them. The Crank was a little worried: his friend is an excellent body repairer, but he was afraid that the damage might be more serious than he had thought. A damaged body affects road-holding, so it is absolutely imperative that all the panels, particularly the lower ones and the base, should be re-squared. The Crank hasn't the necessary equipment for this sort of work, which needs special equipment—a rigid framework of the same dimensions as the body. It reproduces the exact contours of the base.

At first glance, the Crank and Robert saw that Saumer had done them proud. Two workmen had been working furiously on Ferblantine and old Bricard's brief examination was conclusive. When the body came back from Vitry, it would be as good as new.

May 24th

Saumer has phoned up to ask Robert to take over Ferblantine's seats, so that the body repairer can put them in position before he repaints the body. He has also asked if we want to keep the original coral. After a discussion, we decided that Ferblantine should stay the same, but with a white band, four inches in width, running along the middle of her bonnet and roof. Tomorrow morning I shall accompany Robert to Virty before going to the office.

May 25th

We left early this morning. The Crank stayed in bed. Robert and I met at the garage, where we loaded the two seats into Rosalie. We suddenly discovered to our horror that one of the seats had a stain. Someone had carelessly upset about a quarter of a pint of oil on it.

Robert was very put out: it would indeed have been a pity to put a dirty fitting in a nice clean car. We were bewailing the fact when we suddenly realized what dopes we were; there was the seat the thief had left and that Robert had turned into an armchair. We therefore stopped at the Daroux' house and exchanged them. Apart from this little setback, everything has gone fine. Saumer has promised to deliver Ferblantine's newly painted body himself in two days' time.

May 26th

Jules Langlois is a funny character. After enthusiastically agreeing to stay on at the Garage de l'Avenir, he let it be known, this week, that it was highly likely he would be leaving us sooner than expected. He had been offered a job nearer where he was living at Champigny. Now he has changed his mind again: he's not going. He announced his decision with such a tragic air that you might have thought he was being imprisoned in the Garage de l'Avenir. Whatever Robert may say, I find him more and more unpleasant. I can't stand fickle people. Yesterday evening, for instance, he asked Robert if he could let him have the seat from the Dauphine he had at home. One of his pals had asked him for one, as his own was broken. This particular pal was broke at the moment and didn't want to go to any expense. Robert very kindly offered it to him for nothing . . . We had both forgotten that morning's incident. Then Robert remembered and warned Jules that he had had to switch them.

"It's stained," he said, "but you can use it. Your pal will only have to put a cover on it. It's still better than a broken seat!"

You should have seen Jules' face. You would have thought Robert had insulted him personally because he had changed the stained seat. After complaining away for an hour about this wretched seat he seemed to lose all interest. At six o'clock, when he was about to leave the garage to go back to Champigny, Robert suggested he drop by his place to pick up the thing. And all Jules said was that there was no hurry and he'd see about it another time . . .!

May 28th

I have at last seen the famous Sherlock Holmes whom Monsieur Médor was talking about the other day. I've been going mad for two days: there has been a pile of work in the office and a mass of family obligations (Auntie has had to go to the hospital), so I was not able to go to the garage. Yesterday Robert phoned to tell me that Saumer had delivered Ferblantine and that I just must see her! So that afternoon, as I had an errand to do for the office at Plessis, I dashed round to the Rue Bon-Repos. Robert and the Crank were out. They had gone off after lunch to a scrap yard to get some part or other. When I got there, a Citroën, a D.S. 19, was parked outside the garage. Standing there were Jules, Madame Bricard and a customer, the owner of the D.S. 19. Madame Bricard seemed upset. She was in the Crank's so-called office, rummaging among the papers and protesting that she was not mad. Jules, on the other hand, was swearing that he was certain Monsieur Bricard had taken "it" into the house that morning. To which Adèle replied, as she turned everything upside down, that *she* had not seen "it". Eventually I grasped that what they were looking for so feverishly was a catalogue. Ten minutes previously the gentleman with the D.S. 19 had stopped in front of the door and asked if someone could check his ignition, which was not functioning properly. Jules had quickly found out what was wrong. It was the distributor; the condenser was not working. He had therefore changed it and had asked Madame Bricard the price. At the time Adèle was in that rabbit hutch of an office doing the accounts. She had looked for the catalogue to find out the price. No catalogue. It was a sharpish exchange because Madame Bricard said she had seen the price list an hour before in the rabbit hutch, whereas Jules maintained that the Crank had taken it into the house.

The customer waited for the argument to come to an end and stood looking at Ferblantine, standing in a corner on jacks. Although he looked calm enough, he was nonetheless put out. It is always embarrassing to be a spectator at that sort of stupid argument.

"Lovely, isn't she," I could not help saying to him as he was intently examining the body, studying every detail like a person who is *really* interested.

He nodded in agreement and stood back. I did not insist. The owner of the D.S. 19 did not want to talk. I settled down to admiring Ferblantine.

At the other end of the garage the argument had died down. Adèle had decided to go into the house an see if by any chance that old muddlehead of a Crank had not hidden the catalogue there.

"You ought to go and help her," Jules said.

He was scarlet with rage. I noticed that his hands were shaking.

I protested that Adèle wouldn't greet me with cries of joy if I went snooping about in her house, even with the object of helping her.

The mechanic gave a despairing look at the customer over my shoulder.

"I'm s-sorry," he stammered. "It's just one of those things. I can't help it."

The scene with Adèle had really upset Jules. He was all a-dither.

"Very well," the customer said.

I jumped and spun round. I thought he was three yards away. He was just behind me. He was staring straight through me as though he was thinking of something else, and something he did not like, at that. I felt most uncomfortable.

At that moment the asthmatic wheeze of a 2 CV rooted us to the spot. The car had stopped. We looked slowly towards the street. A man got out of the little Citroën. Coming in out of the bright sunlight, he blinked as he tried to accustom his eyes to the darkness of the barn and see if anyone was there.

Jules went forward.

The new arrival was a medium-sized man, stoutish and wearing a tweed suit. His short fair hair, easy gait and open face gave him a sporty look. One took to him at once.

"I don't know what's gone wrong," he said, after nodding towards each of us in turn, but my little buggy's acting funny. She starts up all right, but as soon as I put my foot on the accelerator the engine splutters and I can't go 200 yards without stalling!"

"The carburettor jet must be blocked," grumbled Jules.

The other gave him a cheerful smile.

"I suppose in that case it will have to be unblocked . . . Could you do it immediately or will I have to leave the car?"

"Why not?" said the owner of the D.S. 19, whose opinion had not been asked. "He has finished with me . . . In this place," he added amiably, "they're quick on the job, but it takes time to get to pay for it."

He seemed suddenly quite relaxed.

Jules shrugged resignedly, lifted up the car's bonnet and half disappeared inside.

Adèle Bricard came storming out of the little door at the back of the garage. Far from being appeased, she was even more angry. The catalogue wasn't in the house. Jules had been seeing things and had made her look all for nothing.

The mechanic looked daggers at her, but couldn't say anything as he had taken out the jet and was blowing through it.

The owner of the D.S. 19 handed a ten-franc note to Madame Bricard.

"It's not worth worrying about," he said. "A condenser must cost five francs at the most. You pay for it and give the change to your mechanic as his tip . . ."

Adèle protested. It was far too much! Ten francs, including the tip, for such a little job! But the client refused to argue, got back into his car and shot off.

"If you're in a hurry," Jules said to the owner of the 2 CV, "just unblocking the jet will be enough. If you're not, it would be better to clean out the carburettor."

"Oh, clean it—clean it!" the other exclaimed. "I've bags of time."

His reply reminded me that I had not. I took a hurried farewell.

At the end of the Rue Bon-Repos, I passed Monsieur Médor's café. He beckoned to me discreetly.

"So he came in the end!" he said, dragging me by the arm behind the little spindle trees on the terrace so that we should not be seen.

I looked at him in bewilderment. Who or what was he talking about?

"The policeman, of course! The self-styled travelling salesman! He would sit right here scribbling away. From time to time he would look up as though he were thinking . . . But I've got eyes in my head, I know. He was watching the garage . . . When the D.S. 19 arrived, he put away his things and went off down the Rue Lécureur. He keeps his car there—although there's lots of room here. There's something fishy going on . . . Five minutes later he drove past. His 2 CV was hiccupping . . . he must have done something to it . . . You know enough about engines, Monsieur Serge, to know there's nothing easier . . . It was an excuse to stop at the garage . . . What was that D.S. 19 there for? You must know. You saw it. And what was that Jules doing?"

As gently as possible I managed to get old Médor back behind his bar. When he understood that I would not talk—because I had nothing to say—he let me go. I saw him take up a thriller he had left on a chair. I managed to read the title: *A body in the boot.* Poor old Médor. If he goes on like that, he'll end up in a padded cell.

❀ ❀ 7 ❀ ❀

THERE SHE WAS, STANDING on her four wheels, with her nose towards the street, ready for fresh adventures. She looked brand-new, with dazzling chromium and a glittering coat of coral paint.

"Isn't she beautiful!" sighed Robert Darous. The circle of Ferblantine's admirers nodded in perfect unison. They consisted of the Crank, Adèle, Serge, Jules, Jean and Robert. They stood there, fascinated, seized with a kind of timidity in front of this jewel, although they knew her every bolt.

After all those days of feverish work, there was the car as they had dreamed her. A few seconds more and the spell would be broken. Ferblantine's wheels would turn for the first time and she would be living another life . . . Never again would it be quite like this.

"Well," said the Crank, in tones of emotion, "it's your move, Robert Daroux . . ." Robert stepped forward, opened the door and sat down behind the wheel. He placed his hands lovingly on that ring of plastic and settled down into the seat. He was going to take his time—and relish every gesture. He was taking possession.

In spite of his hard-boiled air, the Crank was a sentimental old thing at heart. By a sort of tacit agreement with Robert, another big softy, he had carried out the final road checks. Because of that, the young mechanic had not taken the wheel of the car . . . He found himself paradoxically in the position of an ordinary customer who on the appointed day comes to take delivery of a Dauphine straight from the factory.

"Go on, take her away!" cried Jules. "You won't break her!"

The marmoset had none of those finer feelings. Furthermore, he was somewhat flushed, as during the morning he had paid one or two lightning visits to Monsieur Médor. "Is it hot!" he exclaimed each time when the Crank gave him a sideways look, "I could drink the sea and all the little fishes . . ."

It was certainly a fine day, but it must be admitted that Jules' actions, the last few days, had been most peculiar. The nearer Ferblantine came to completion, the more nervous he became. The former wreck exercised an inexplicable fascination over him. During the past week he must have asked a hundred times on what day she would be ready. He had made a tremendous fuss when they discovered there was a leak in the radiator, a tiny hole through which the water destined to cool the engine was escaping drop by drop.

"I knew it!" he said. "I pointed out that scratch on the engine. No one bothered to check. That's another day lost!"

"Pooh!" exclaimed the Crank. "Only a hole in the radiator? That's nothing. In the 1934 Twenty-four Hours at Le Mans, the fuel tank in Philippe Etancelin's and Louis Chinetti's Alfa-Romeo burst after only a few hours on the track. There was no question of repairing it properly, but we had to plug up the hole somehow. We collected every bit of chewing gum we could find in the area and all started chewing that damn rubber stuff. Every time the Alfa stopped we plugged the tank with wads of the muck. And Etancelin and Chinetti won! But we poor mechanics had stiff jaws for days afterwards."

In spite of everything, the Crank had gone off to look for a new radiator and the day had been lost. "We'll lose a lot more yet," he said to Robert, who, without being as impatient as Jules, was dying to take the wheel. The garage owner was referring to the mechanical snags they had come up against. Bricard and his mechanic had been thinking of making very considerable modifications to Ferblantine's engine. Very soon, however, they had agreed that the work involved would mean putting off Ferblantine's first outing for several weeks. Consequently, the Crank, with the approval of the others, had bought a Dauphine engine from a friend. They were to experiment on this engine on a bench in one corner of the garage, and when it was just as they wanted it, it would go into Ferblantine.

"In the meantime," the Crank had said, "you can get your hand in with the present engine. You drive all right, but you've still a few things to learn . . . We'll get down to them . . ."

Although Robert was longing to become a champion in the near future, his immediate passion was to take over his own car—so it was with an excitement as intense as though the engine had been "souped up" that he took his seat behind Ferblantine's wheel.

He turned the ignition starter key (there is just the one switch on a Dauphine) and the engine roared into life. Serge took his seat next to his friend. It was the co-driver's, the navigator's seat, the one he would soon be occupying in a competition. Jean Daroux got into the back.

Adèle was standing at the garage door looking out into the street. With a broad gesture she signalled that the road was clear. Robert got into first, let off the handbrake and gently let in his clutch . . . Ferblantine moved imperceptibly forward.

"See you soon!" called out the Crank. "Don't do anything silly!"

Robert drove slowly out of the garage, turned right, accelerated slightly and changed into second. In his mirror he could see the Bricards and Jules waving their hands. Sitting out on the terrace of his café, Monsieur Médor was chatting idly with a customer.

"Look at that!" said Serge, laughing. "Monsieur Médor is still being pumped by his Sherlock Holmes!"

He had just recognized the customer in conversation with the café keeper. It was the man in the 2 CV.

Robert was already turning left into the Avenue de la République. His thoughts were a thousand miles away from Médor's Sherlock Holmes.

"Dad's going to get a surprise!" he chuckled.

"So's Mum!" echoed Jean.

The two brothers had thought of an idea which did credit to their natures and to their diplomatic skill. Ferblantine, as has been said, was not on very good terms with the Daroux family. From the very first, Madame Daroux had announced that she "just couldn't bear the thought of her son at the wheel". His father had not gone quite so far: he could accept the fact that Robert would one day drive a car like so many others—"one must move with the times"—but forgetting that he had himself once dreamed occasionally of seeing his son become a champion racing driver, he did not hide his prejudice against competitions. So as to avoid further argument, no one mentioned Ferblantine when the family was all together. That could not go on for ever, Robert and Jean felt. Their parents would have to overcome their reticence . . . Ferblantine herself would have to win their hearts!

"We must attack Dad," Jean had said. "He's really thrilled you've got a car . . . What he's frightened of now is that you want to be a racing driver . . . You haven't come to that yet. He's the only one who can make Mum see that there's nothing unusual about driving an ordinary car . . ."

They had looked for the best way to get their father on their side. Serge, who had taken part in this little plot, had insisted that they had to find a "gun that fires round corners" ploy.

"I'll explain," he had added. "It's your mother you should aim at—*through* your father."

Robert had thought a moment. Then his face had cleared.

"This is what we'll do for Ferblantine's first run . . ."

After leaving Le Plessis, Robert set off in the direction of the Villeneuve-Saint-Georges marshalling yard. Monsieur Daroux was working on repairs to the track there.

That particular week he finished work at 2 p.m. At five to two, the Dauphine stopped in front of the little door he would leave by.

Three pairs of eyes were glued to it.

A minute to two . . . two o'clock . . . a minute past . . .

A man came through the door, then two men, then a number of them . . . Most of them were in their working clothes; some were running to catch their bus.

"Here he is," Jean whispered.

Monsieur Daroux appeared in the middle of a little group that stopped just outside the door. They all shook hands.

"Psst!" hissed Serge, putting his head out through the window. The workmen all turned round. Monsieur Daroux recognized his sons' friend.

"Hello!" he said, mildly surprised.

He still had not connected him with the car . . .

"Why, it's my boys!" he exclaimed at last. He bent at the knees to see them better.

"We came to fetch you," said Robert, opening the door.

Jean got out next, followed by Serge.

"It's her first run," was all Robert said, pointing to Ferblantine. "We thought you might like . . ."

A face tanned and creased by day upon day of rain and sun out on the tracks crinkled up with delight. Monsieur Daroux was very pleased indeed.

"They're my sons," he said to his friends, who were all following the scene: they were visibly impressed by Daroux's lads. He added with pride:

"This is the car I was telling you about. It was my eldest, Robert, who rebuilt it."

Monsieur Daroux might observe a total silence on the subject of Ferblantine at home, but that did not prevent his talking about her all the time to his friends at work! The three young people could not help smiling at this involuntary admission. And Monsieur Daroux smiled, too, with a mixture of guilt and complicity.

"Isn't she a beauty!" he said as he examined her. "She's brand-new!"

"You wait till you hear the engine," exclaimed Jean enthusiastically. "She goes like a bird!"

Serge kindly insisted on Monsieur Daroux sitting in front, next to the driver. The railwayman got in awkwardly, with clumsy gestures.

"A car's certainly a nice thing to have," he said, when Ferblantine had barely gone 500 yards.

He was happy and relaxed. He smiled as he looked

at the pedestrians, of whom all he could see was their feet. Robert passed a bus and his father exclaimed, "Isn't it big!" He saw people and things from a different angle. The streets he walked daily seemed strange to him. He found it hard to recognize his usual landmarks: particular bus stops, particular tobacconists . . .

"You drive all right," he said with conviction as his eldest son drew up smoothly at a red light.

"He's a champ!" cried Jean.

They all laughed. Monsieur Daroux was on their side.

Madame Daroux was in her kitchen when a gentle toot on the horn made her look up. A car had stopped in front of the door. Someone was waving an arm through the window. Then a head replaced the arm.

"Etienne!" she said, recognizing her husband.

That same second she realized that this Dauphine was her son's and that its crew had gone to wait for her husband as he left work. Besides, they were all now getting out with a great banging of doors.

"They are good boys, I must say," she thought. "They went to fetch him."

Victory was theirs. Robert had been right. He knew that his mother would hardly weaken at the sight of a glittering Ferblantine, but she *was* touched that the children should think of their father the first time they went out in the car.

Monsieur Daroux was putting a bold face on it, but he was a bit uneasy and waited for his wife's reaction. Berthe could be obstinate. It would be very aggravating if she really was against this car. It would upset the family. After all, Robert was grown up . . . Rallies are not the same thing as track races. From out of the corner of his eye, Monsieur Daroux was observing his wife. Was she going to come out of the cottage and meet them? If she did not, it was a bad omen.

Madame Daroux disappeared from the window and reappeared in the little garden between the house and the street. She came towards the little group, towards Ferblantine.

"Well," she said to her husband, "you did come home in style."

It was easy to determine from her tone of voice that she was putting up a fight, that she had not yet completely given up the struggle. Two opposing feelings warred within her . . . She shot a critical glance at Ferblantine, glowing in the sun. It was true that she "still could not bear the thought" . . . but they all looked so happy!

She mechanically wiped a little spot off the bodywork.

"You have worked hard," she said to Robert. "You're happy, you deserve it . . . That's the main thing."

The men breathed a discreet sigh of relief. The battle was won! Ferblantine was one of the family!

A delighted Monsieur Daroux dragged them all into the cottage. A day like this called for a drink!

As though by magic, the street, which a few minutes before had been deserted was suddenly full of people. A Sioux tribe of some ten boys had left the warpath to cluster round Ferblantine; they felt a kind of proprietary interest in her. After all, Robert and Jean Daroux might be a good bit older but they were still more or less their kind . . . Did not the grown-ups, the adults talk of them as "the children"?

"That wasn't fair!" their chief, a boy named Popaul, shouted to Robert, who was leaning out of the window to watch the Sioux's antics. "You promised to tell us when you were taking her out on her first run! We helped you, didn't we? Popaul was recalling a vague promise. As for his gang's part in assembling Ferblantine, that consisted in having twice gone to buy cigarettes for the Crank.

"She's great!" exclaimed another of the kids. "You can see she's being prepared for racing: she's been underslung."

He had a sharp eye. Monsieur Daroux, who could hear everything from the cottage dining-room, winked at his son.

"He's smarter than me. I hadn't noticed it."

"It was the Crank who modified the suspension: it will improve her road-holding."

"They'll scratch the paint, you know," fussed Madame Daroux. "They are all over it like flies round a honeypot."

"He was like that at their age," the father said with an indulgent smile. "Do you remember? As soon as you saw a car you had to prowl round it."

"You leave it alone!" Madame Daroux called out to the children. "Be off with you!"

They were slyly trying the door handles. A moment later they had opened them and were lolling about the seats . . .

"Listen, kids," Robert intervened. "I'm going back to the garage. Wait for me there and I promise I'll give you a ride."

A howl of joy greeted this news.

"Forward!" cried Popaul, the Sioux chief.

And with the tribe at his heels, he galloped off in the direction of the nearby Rue Bon-Repos.

"Why did you say that to them?" scolded Madame Daroux. "They'll dirty the cushions!"

"I think I'd have liked someone to say that to me when I was their age," said Robert reflectively.

A few minutes later, Ferblantine stopped in front of the Garage de l'Avenir. The door was shut and the

Sioux were waiting outside, looking perplexed. Robert saw the Crank standing outside Monsieur Médor's café, signalling to him to come and join him.

"I have a feeling," Serge said, "that Jules has managed to drag the Crank over there . . . they must be celebrating the happy event."

Serge was wrong. Jules was not directly responsible for the Crank's breaking his sacred principle of not propping up bars. What had happened was that the mechanic, burning with an inner fire, had told the café keeper in the course of one of his lightning visits that it was a great day because Ferblantine was taking the road for the first time. Monsieur Médor, in a sudden fit of generosity, had insisted on the garage owner and Madame Bricard coming over to celebrate at his establishment. It was his contribution to the general rejoicing.

The Bricards had let themselves be persuaded . . .

"We were waiting for you to come back," the Crank said to the young people, "before raising our glasses." Then he added, "What do those kids want?" pointing at the boys who had come trotting up in the car's wake.

"Robert has promised them a ride," explained Jean.

"All right, but in a minute . . . We must have a drink with Médor first or he'll be upset."

The café keeper had ceremoniously arranged a row of glasses on the bar. At that time the place was deserted. There was only one customer, the man with a crew-cut and the 2 CV, who Médor insisted was a policeman. He had joined them without being asked and never stopped expressing his admiration at their transforming a wreck into a gleaming limousine.

"We get by," said the Crank, bridling with pleasure. "Robert is still only a youngster but he's got it there . . ."

"To think that when I first knew him he couldn't even walk!" exclaimed Médor with emotion.

Popaul and his Indians had slipped into the café and were keeping a close guard on Robert.

"Come on now, out of here!" bellowed the café keeper.

"We're waiting for Robert! He promised!"

"All right, but you must keep quiet! I'll bring you some lemonades out to the terrace. And then you'll leave us in peace!"

And Médor, who indeed had a fit of generosity on him, did as he promised.

They all chattered away. Jules, who was growing thirstier and thirstier, told the story, illustrated with hideous grimaces, of his apprenticeship. His sole audience consisted of Madame Bricard, who listened politely. The others were listening open-mouthed to the tale of Ferblantine's adventure, told by the Crank.

"It's a real fairy story," wheezed Monsieur Médor.

"What a wonderful example!" exclaimed the fake police officer.

They had discovered that he was called Rambaud and sold underwear. His present area was the south-eastern suburbs and part of Seine-et-Marne. That was why he had more or less settled in Le Plessis.

Out on the terrace the boys were sipping their fizzy lemonade. They all had their heads turned towards the bar and were intently listening to the story of Ferblantine.

The Crank was in full spate and literally holding the audience under his spell. Jules, who was having difficulty with his speech, had given up telling the tale of his youth. He had collapsed onto a chair in front of the door . . . Half hidden behind the spindle trees, and parked beside the pavement, the coral Dauphine waited patiently.

"And that isn't all!" the Crank was saying. "Do you know where we found the special springs for the suspension?"

But this question, dramatic though it was, was to remain unanswered.

One of the kids cried out:

"Robert, there's a man getting into your car!"

Robert was sitting with his back to the spindles. He heard a noise, turned round and . . .

The appearance of a dinosaur in Médor's establishment would not have had such an effect.

The Crank sat open-mouthed. The others were hypnotized.

"There's-a-man-getting-into-your-car."

"WHAT!" roared a dozen pairs of lungs.

At that moment an engine started up. *Ferblantine's engine*!

There was a stampede. They had understood at last! Some unspeakable swine was in the act of stealing the car.

Jules was sitting astride his chair in front of the entrance. When the little boy cried out he got up, a slightly wavering obstacle but nonetheless an obstacle. The stampede passed over him for one, maybe two, seconds. The Crank, Robert, Jean, Serge, Médor and Rambaud poured out on to the pavement to see Ferblantine go by.

In first gear, with the accelerator hard down, the thief roared past.

8

IN THE HANDS OF her abductor, Ferblantine forged straight ahead. In a group on the pavement, in front of Monsieur Médor's establishment, the Crank and his wife, Jean, Serge, Robert, Jules, Rambaud the salesman, and the ten or so Sioux of Popaul's gang joined their voices in a bellow in which distress and rage mingled with indignation.

Ferblantine turned up a one-way street.

At the moment when this tragic tale begins to unfold, it would be a good idea for the spectator to rise above this humble district of the worthy town of Le Plessis. He will overlook the maze of streets and without raising a single roof will be able to understand the subtleties of the drama that is about to be enacted.

Seated in mid-air, he will see first of all the Rue Bon-Repos with its Garage de l'Avenir and its anonymous café. Just beyond the latter, the important Avenue de la République cuts across the Rue Bon-Repos, which changes its name after crossing the Avenue. For a hundred yards it becomes the Rue des Tilleuls. When it has covered its hundred yards of cobbles, the Rue des Tilleuls meets at a right angle a narrow street of shops called the Rue du Vieux-Marché and then continues its way between two blocks of flats under the name of the Rue des Acacias. The Avenue de la République and the Rue du Vieux-Marché both exit at their eastern ends into a large main street called the Rue Nationale, which is used by vehicles travelling to or from Paris. As everyone knows, these "one-way streets", a modern invention intended to channel an excess of traffic, are multiplying daily in the capital of France. The worthy councillors of Plessis, unable to afford an Eiffel Tower to rival the metropolis, had managed, of recent months, to multiply *their* one-way streets. Red discs with white bars therefore decorated the Rue des Tilleuls and the Rue des Acacias, forbidding their use from south to north. The Rue du Vieux-Marché on the other hand denied passage to vehicles travelling from east to west.

It was obvious that the man who had stolen Ferblantine was ignorant of these important topographical details; excitement must have made him forget to check that he did not break both the highway code and the local by-laws. Ignoring the Avenue de la République, he drove straight ahead . . .

The shout of horror raised by the Crank and his friends served to condemn both the infamous theft of Ferblantine and the infringement of the law.

Two words that burst out from nearly twenty breasts rang in the ears of passers-by for hundreds of yards: "STOP, THIEF!"

People often speak, and rightly, of the magic of words. The two syllables "Stop, thief" crossed the Avenue de la République, plunged down the Rue des Tilleuls and overtook the coral Dauphine. The fastest of cars cannot compete with the speed of sound.

The thief had barely started down the Rue des Tilleuls when the two magic syllables lodged in the two ears most suited to receive them. They belonged to Gendarme Tropinet whom chance and the duty of returning an army pay book to a soldier-citizen of Le Plessis had brought to the junction of the Rue des Tilleuls and the Rue du Vieux-Marché. The sharp eye of fisherman Tropinet summed up the situation in a flash. This Dauphine was travelling at speed in the wrong direction down a one-way street and a distant chorus was voicing the lamentations of those who have been robbed!

The driver of the vehicle was breaking the highway code and also, it appeared, the penal code . . . Gendarme Tropinet dashed off, waving his arms in the air . . .

The thief saw the guardian of law and order about to fling himself literally onto his bonnet. He jammed on his brakes, flung over the wheel to the right, just brushed Tropinet . . . and stalled his engine. For a second fate hesitated . . . It only wanted Tropinet to jump forward and drag the scoundrel from his seat. Had he done so, the adventure would have stopped there, at the junction of the Rue du Vieux-Marché and the Rue des Tilleuls . . .

The gendarme failed to leap. Brushed by Ferblantine's front left wing, he spun round and sat down with a bump, suddenly realizing, to his horror, what a narrow squeak he had had . . . He needed three seconds to realize that he was safe, that his duty bade him go on to the bitter end. He got up. But, alas, it was too late. The thief had taken only two seconds to decide that he should continue his journey as soon as possible. The engine roared again. The car leaped forward. At that very moment the villain saw the one-way sign forbidding him to go on straight ahead down the Rue des Acacias. He stopped dead in the middle of the crossroads, just in front of a Peugeot 404 turning out of the Rue du Vieux-Marché. He had only just heard the beginning of the stream of curses pouring out of the Peugeot owner's mouth, when he saw that he could not turn left as there was another sign. He swung right and just mounted the pavement, as he had gone out too far into the middle of the cross-roads . . .

Beaten by one tiny second, Gendarme Tropinet had got up too late. The fugitive's hesitation gave him the chance, however, to make up for his handicap. First, he drew a splendid whistle from his pocket; second, he raised it to his mouth and blew it as hard as he could after the Dauphine . . . The stridency of a "pea" whistle has the virtue of attracting a crowd's attention. The passers-by and the housewives who in that part of the town were going about their daily business had originally thought it was a normal traffic hold-up.

Brakes and tyres squealed, two cars stopped dead, and their air was blue with curses . . . But when they saw the gendarme pop out like a jack-in-the box, whistling like a madman, the onlookers realized that something odd was going on.

From being common spectators, they were in danger of becoming participants. The majority started shouting in all directions: some of them fled—also in all directions.

The gendarme opened the door of the 404. "Follow that car," he cried to the driver, pointing to the coral Dauphine, which already had a thirty yards' start.

"We'll catch him," answered the driver as he let in his clutch.

Tropinet, képi askew, put his head out of the car window and started blowing his whistle again . . .

While this scene from a Western was taking place,

a hundred yards away, the luckless victims of the abduction of Ferblantine had not remained inactive. From a distance, they had seen a man fling himself in front of the Dauphine and fall while the car was about to stop. A wild hope had sent the majority of them dashing forward. The Crank, Serge and the Sioux had run flat out to the crossroads.

Although on that particular day this odd lot of runners beat their own personal records for the hundred-yard dash, they nevertheless arrived too late to take part in the operations . . . Serge, the swiftest, did however arrive in time to see the 404 shoot off like a rocket, bearing with it a whistling Tropinet, modern version of Justice in pursuit of Crime.

Some, therefore, dashed off on foot after Ferblantine. The others, that is to say, Rambaud the underwear salesman, Robert and Jean Daroux, reacted differently.

"He's getting tangled up in the one-ways," cried Rambaud. "We'll get him!"

This elliptical statement meant that the thief—supposing that he continued his flight—would most likely take the Rue du Vieux-Marché to rejoin the Rue Nationale. Taking into account the precious seconds lost and still to lose, there might be a chance of arriving in time to bar his way to the above-mentioned Rue Nationale.

Robert and Jean Daroux understood the salesman's idea.

He had already dived into his 2 CV, which was standing outside the café. Switch—starter—and he was off. Jean and Robert were clinging to the outside. The 2 CV shot out into the Avenue de la République under the nose of a huge truck, narrowly missed a cyclist, passed a bus . . . Rambaud had jammed the horn. The two brothers shouted, "Stop thief! Stop thief! Stop thief!"

They cornered again, this time to the left. Into the heavy traffic of the Rue Nationale. Ignoring the rules, Rambaud overtook a whole column of cars on the left. The continuous blare of the horn and the shouts of his two passengers, who were leaning right over the roof, cleared the road for him.

Suddenly, thirty yards ahead of the 2 CV, Ferblantine shot out of the Rue du Vieux-Marché. Jean and Robert redoubled their yells, while Rambaud stamped on the accelerator. It was a matter of inches! A 404 going like a bomb nearly took off the little car's nose. On his right a gendarme was blowing his whistle . . . Robert, in a flash, recognized Tropinet and the gendarme recognized him.

"It's my car!" shouted the young man. "After him!"

Tropinet, who in a few minutes had twice missed death by a hair's breadth, did not understand. He did more than that, he guessed!

He connected Robert with the Crank. The shouts of "Thief!" came from the Rue Bon-Repos, not far from the Garage de l'Avenir. Robert—Crank—Dauphine—one-way street—Thief. The association of ideas suddenly rang the bell.

"Someone has stolen the Crank's car!" thought Tropinet. Not merely duty but friendship called on him to catch the villian.

"Faster! Sound your horn!" he ordered his volunteer driver.

The latter, only too pleased to be able for once to break the law with impunity, put his foot down and furiously blew the horn. Tropinet returned to blowing his whistle.

The drivers coming in the opposite direction hugged the curb in terror as they saw the three cars bearing down on them. Some of them even mounted the pavement with a screech of brakes.

The desperate chase went on.

Obviously Ferblantine, who luckily was not equipped with a supercharged engine, was outclassed by the 404 in the matter of pure speed. And as for the salesman's 2 CV, she wasn't even in the running. But a chase, however desperate, at five in the evening, in the suburbs, cannot make use of all the horsepower concealed under a car's bonnet. A *slalom* is not a *Schuss*, to use ski-ing parlance. And Ferblantine, with two cars at her heels, was in for a slalom rather than a straight race.

Either he was a brilliant driver or fear made him oblivious of danger, but the thief put up a remarkable performance under the circumstances. A turn to the right, a skid to the left . . . *I can filter here . . . cut in there . . . slip between that bus and the 4 CV . . . lights are green . . . amber . . . RED! Can't be helped, I'm through!* . . . It really was a championship and, in any other circumstances, motorists, passers-by and policemen on point duty would have stared in amazement. Only no one in the section had heard there was to be a sporting event that afternoon. Far from being enthralled, drivers were shouting, braking, stalling and crashing into each other's rears. Passers-by were screaming and cowering in doorways . . . as for the policemen . . .! They were waving their white truncheons in the air and whistling fit to burst their lungs in answer to Gendarme Tropinet's racing solo. Some dashed to the police call-boxes and rang up the local station, "police-emergency", the Home Office, the Fire Brigade and the Gendarmerie.

Ferblantine roared off in a mighty Grand Finale.

When he reached Villiers-sur-Marne, the thief took the Paris road, seeking safety not in open country where a chase at speed would have turned to his disadvantage, but towards the capital, where he hoped to lose his pursuers in the labyrinth of streets. From time to time he saw in his driving mirror the 404 which had the top half of a gendarme sticking out of its right-hand side . . . By taking completely crazy risks, he managed to gain a lead of a hundred yards . . . The 2 CV had disappeared from view. A few spurts at just under 70 m.p.h. had been enough to leave it well behind. Turning off at the end of the road to Villiers, he took the Quai Louis-Ferber, running alongside the Marne, then turned left, crossed the Pont de Bry and shot off through Le Perreux . . . He gave a sigh of relief. A few more zigzags in the town and the 404 would lose the scent . . . There were a lot of little side streets emerging into the Avenue Pierre-Brossolette which he was just going up. He decided to take the second on the right . . . He could see the 404 growing larger in his mirror . . . He double-clutched and went down into second for a fast turn . . . At that moment he saw coming towards him a black Renault Domaine with a tall whip aerial. A police patrol car! At once he knew he had been recognized. A coral Dauphine with a white band down the middle is easily identifiable, particularly when followed by a 404 bearing a whistling gendarme . . . The Domaine drifted slightly over to the left, obviously with the intention of blocking the avenue. He pulled his wheel hard over—and thought for a second that his turn would end in a series of somersaults, but the Dauphine still kept her course. He accelerated. There was another little side street fifty yards ahead on the left. He glanced in his mirror: the police Domaine had also turned down the street By the time he had reached the side street he saw the 404 come in sight, too. Round he went! It was lucky there was nothing coming in the other direction.

Sweat was pouring down the man's face. He was horribly hot—and horribly frightened. He was not worried about the 404. But there were complications. The police had joined in the chase. He knew from experience what would happen next: inside the Domaine a policeman would be giving a running commentary over the radio: "Hello! Hello! Calling all cars! Coral Dauphine seen at Le Perreux! General Call!" In some police station or other, another policeman sitting in front of a microphone would already be organizing the hunt. "Block the bridges over the Marne. Orders for the Nogent and Neuilly detachments . . ." In a few minutes the plan for setting up road blocks would have been set in motion . . . And the others, the Domaine and the 404 were still on his heels! . . . The man cornered, braked, accelerated, went through the gears and turned left and right while he tried to think. However relaxed a driver you are, it is not easy to think under such conditions . . . He still had a chance of making his get-away—on foot. He could slip into a block of flats and escape over the roofs or through the gardens. His followers were not numerous enough to worry him seriously. Before there were enough men to surround the area, he would be far away. What would the boss say? He would be annoyed, but he would understand. "Whatever you do, don't take unnecessary risks," he had warned him.

The man hesitated no longer. He seemed to feel the noose tightening round him. He had just turned again. The Domaine and the 404 would be in sight again within a few seconds. He spotted a block of buildings with carriage doors opening on to inner courtyards. This was the moment.

He jammed on his brakes, opened the door and flung himself into the entrance of the nearest building. There was a shed at the far side of the courtyard. He sprinted.

The courtyard was empty. No one had seen him. He was just reaching the shed when behind him in the street he heard a vehicle screech to a halt. He slipped inside.

The policemen had leaped out of the Domaine, revolvers in their hands. The coral Dauphine had been abandoned. The driver had vanished. The 404 pulled up behind the squad car. Out leaped Gendarme Tropinet followed by the driver.

"Where is he?" they shouted simultaneously.

Inside the Domaine, the radio operator was still giving his commentary.

"The coral Dauphine has stopped in the Rue Nodier. The driver has made a dash for it."

"He must be somewhere in the area," one of the policemen said brightly.

"He must have gone into one of these three buildings," volunteered another. "There are lots of little outhouses off these courtyards. He must be hiding in one of them."

"He may be armed," said a third policeman solemnly.

They all nodded sagely. The squealing brakes and banging doors had brought people to the windows. Concierges were emerging from their basements. A little crowd collected.

"I think we should wait for reinforcements," one of the policemen suggested.

He had sense. They all agreed with him.

Three minutes later a police van arrived full of armed police, then two patrol cars, six motorcycle policemen, two superintendents and five plainclothes inspectors.

Investigations were opened . . .

While the man who had stolen Ferblantine was enjoying his freedom at Le Perreux, Robert, Jean and

Rambaud, the underwear salesman, were searching the streets of Bry-sur-Marne for the coral Dauphine and the 404 carrying Tropinet. They had dropped behind in the Rue de Paris at Villiers-sur-Marne, where far ahead of them they had seen Ferblantine and the 404 turn right towards the river. An untimely red light had brought them to a halt. By the time they had been able to start off again, the two cars had vanished from sight.

"I imagine," Rambaud said, "that the thief has disappeared into the streets of Bry. It's an ideal place to lose a pursuer."

They had therefore taken a chance and gone straight ahead. After a good quarter of an hour's search they had to give up. Bry-sur-Marne was enjoying a peaceful afternoon untroubled by the desperate chase or Tropinet's whistle.

"Perhaps the police have been informed," the salesman said, stopping in front of the station.

He came out again five minutes later.

"If we're to believe them," he said, "they have found your car at Le Perreux."

They went off in that direction and, after driving around there for fifteen minutes or so, had the good luck to meet a police car bowling along at top speed. They followed it and finally reached the Rue Nodier.

Surrounded by dark blue uniforms stood Ferblantine with Tropinet at her side.

It is a well-known fact that it is much easier to have something stolen than to retrieve it when the thief has let it fall into the hands of the police. In the general confusion, the two superintendents and the five inspectors leading the attack launched by the forces of law and order on the three buildings first of all thought that Robert was the thief. Tropinet had to produce his papers to prove he was not a fake gendarme. By the time he had got out his wallet and explained how and why he happened to be there, Robert had disappeared and so had Jean and Rambaud. He found them again in the police van under guard. They were about to be taken to the station. Tropinet exploded and explained all over again.

The policemen finally admitted that the Dauphine was the property of Monsieur Robert Daroux, although that was a minor detail to them. For the moment all they were interested in was the thief. The latter was nowhere to be found. After fifty policemen had searched the block with a fine-tooth comb and it was established that the man had made his escape on foot, Jean, Robert and Rambaud were told that they should report to the station to make a statement. Finally, at half-past seven that evening, Ferblantine, at last restored to her rightful owner, stopped in front of Monsieur Médor's café. Out stepped a small, voiceless group of people: Robert, Tropinet, Jean and Serge, who, in response to a telephone call, had rushed to the police station at Le Perreux, together with the Crank.

This last, also voiceless, struggled out of Rosalie, while Monsieur Rambaud, in the same condition, emerged from his 2 CV.

Monsieur Médor was absolutely delighted. He had never known such a wonderful day. It was better than any thriller.

And although they had all lost their voices they had to talk yet again.

"What is your opinion, Monsieur Rambaud?" Médor asked the travelling salesman when he had been told the whole story.

While asking the question, he shot a significant look at the Crank and the three young people. It would be interesting to know what the supposed Sherlock Holmes thought.

"My opinion," the other answered, "is that Robert was darned lucky. If the gendarme hadn't been there, he might as well have said goodbye to his car."

Monsieur Médor could not hide his disappointment. The supposed plain-clothes detective's thoughts were not remarkable for their originality.

He tried again . . .

"What puzzles me is that a thief should have been foolish enough to steal the car here, in such a quiet street. He must have known he would be spotted at once!"

Monsieur Médor's comment was not so stupid.

"Yes, that's true!" exclaimed the Crank. "He must have been a beginner . . . The old hands always work where there are a lot of cars together . . ."

"Besides," went on the café keeper, watching the effect of his words on Rambaud, "you must admit that your Ferblantine attracts thieves. The other week, when you were attacked, it was to steal one of her seats!"

The Crank protested. Ferblantine was pure and innocent!

"You must be right," the salesman said, "but don't forget: everything goes in threes!"

Robert's face dropped. He was not superstitious, but Médor and Rambaud with their theories and suppositions were beginning to make him wonder. Why *was* everything concentrating round Ferblantine?

The Crank reassured him:

"Come, stop worrying! Nothing more will happen now!"

"We'll keep our eyes open," Rambaud said with a laugh.

"That's right, we'll keep our eyes open!" repeated Médor.

And he winked heavily at the Crank, as though to say, "Didn't I say so? He's showing his hand now! Of course he'll keep his eyes open: what else has he been doing since he came snooping round these parts?"

"Where's your mechanic, Jules, gone?" Rambaud asked suddenly, becoming aware of the marmoset's absence.

Bricard's face clouded over. Jules' actions throughout the day had displeased him. He had drunk more than usual.

"He cleared off," he said, "just after you went after Ferblantine. He couldn't stand upright . . . He said he felt sleepy . . . Besides, something tells me that he may very well have gone for good . . . If he *does* come back and goes on like that, I'll sack him."

The salesman nodded understandingly.

"It would be like him to leave without giving any explanations," he said. "But I have a feeling he'll be back."

Then he added casually, as though he attached no importance to what he was saying:

"As for sacking him, I think you'd be making a mistake. Better the devil you know . . ."

✻ ✻ 9 ✻ ✻

EXTRACTS FROM A LETTER from Jean Daroux to his cousin, Olivier Daroux, Lance-corporal in the 3rd Cuirassiers.

"Dear Oli . . .

Ferblantine is doing fine! Peace reigns. I needn't tell you that since the attempt to pinch her, we have been watching over her like hawks . . .

The Crank has decided to devote three hours a day to training the future champion and Serge, his future navigator. Incidentally, you wouldn't recognize the Crank: Ferblantine has given him a second youth. Do you know that so as not to lose a day he decided not to go to Le Mans for the Twenty-four Hours! It will be the first time since they first held the race that Auguste Bricard has not been on the track. He said, 'I'll be seeing enough races with the two kids in them.' Oh, by the way, I forgot to tell you: the Daroux-Rivois team makes its first official appearance in two weeks' time! There's a little rally organized by the Automobile Club de l'Ile de France: the Brie Rally. Our two champions and their manager are entering for it without any illusions. It's just a question of getting their hand in and trying out Ferblantine's modified engine. You can imagine our little team is working like fury with this coming up. Serge is glued to his maps and his timetable. Last Sunday, Robert and he suddenly decided to go and look at the course. They should have been working on Ferblantine, but the Crank had visitors, some relations he had not seen for two years. He was a bit cross at having to lose a day. Anyway, Robert and Serge took advantage of it to make a recce. Naturally I was included in the party. It gave me the chance to see the team in action. I'm sure that once they've been broken in, our two characters will be hot stuff.

Serge had studied his route on the map. As the course is usually over little-known roads, he had worked on large-scale ordnance survey maps which give more detail than the road maps. You know the principle of a rally? It consists of covering a certain distance at an average speed fixed in advance. For the Brie Rally, Ferblantine will have to keep up an average speed of 40 m.p.h., which doesn't look difficult on paper, but represents a pretty good performance on the ground. When you go from, say, Paris to Lyons, keeping to the main roads, there's practically no risk of making a mistake, but when, on the other hand, you get off the highroads it's extraordinary how easy it is to lose your way. On Sunday, for example, we reached a little village where half a dozen minor roads branched off. Serge had made a note that the road we should take out of the village would be the third on the right. Robert slowed down and we all stared . . . It was a fair day! The streets were blocked, there were merry-go-rounds and booths at every crossroad. We started counting . . . one . . . two . . . three . . . We couldn't see a street sign, but then it might be hidden by one of the booths, we thought, and anyway, it *was* the third.

We drove on and on . . . At last we came to a crossroads where we found out we had made a mistake. We had covered four miles in the wrong direction. Back we went to the village. We made enquiries and eventually found out the cause of our error: a huge merry-go-round had been set up in the middle of the street we should have taken. The council had put up a notice showing there was a detour, but it was at the entrance to the first turning we had passed and was half hidden by a parked car. During the actual rally, a mistake of that kind would have cost us dear. The twenty minutes we lost would have lowered our average speed disastrously. It is at a time like that you realize how essential it is for a team to work together perfectly. As the navigator, Serge was responsible, not for the original error, but for continuing in it. He had not studied his map well enough. He should have spotted that the road we ought to have taken went through a forest when it left the village, whereas the one we had taken ran alongside a little river. If he had spotted it, we should have gone only a few hundred yards in the wrong direction and not the four miles we drove in actual fact. He himself realized that at once. Robert and he behaved very well. There were no recriminations. When I pulled Serge's leg about his mistake, Robert said, 'Serge is like me, he's only a beginner . . . And even when we have more experience, it won't prevent us having more incidents of this sort. We must learn to accept them philosophically and have faith in each other. The driver must absolutely never question his navigator's directions, nor must the latter criticize his companion's driving.' That Sunday afternoon we weren't able to cover the whole course Ferblantine will have to cover. We did half of it. I can promise you we didn't waste time mucking about on the way: we behaved as though it was the rally. Even so, we were nowhere near the 40 m.p.h. required. And there was I thinking that rally driving was a peaceful sport. When we got back, our three faces were a mile long. The Crank had to revive our morale.

I should add that, at the moment, the Crank is only interested in the mechanical aspect of the business and in the training. He has in fact set up as a racing instructor and I must admit he's an ace!

Nearly every day, leaving Jules the Marmoset in the garage (he came back two days after his remarkable exhibition in Monsieur Médor's establishment), Bricard took us out to a place not far from Ozoir for training. There was a recently abandoned quarry which offered a flat surface of several acres of clay soil, well beaten down. The result was a superb skating rink which gave Robert—and equally Serge—a chance to learn to skid. You see, a skid, which terrifies people, isn't what the layman thinks. When under control it is to driving what salt is to cooking. A driver worthy of the name could not do without it. To borrow from the vocabulary of the kitchen, it is fantastic how many condiments a man really able to drive can use.

Controlled skidding is the Crank's masterpiece. I suspect him of taking us to the quarry for the pleasure of seeing his colts spinning round on the claylike soil at the wheel of Ferblantine. Robert had some experience of the art before coming out for training, but Serge, although he understood the principle, had never seen it in practice. At each session, Robert let me take the wheel for a quarter of an hour, as he wants me to use the opportunity to learn how to drive properly. The Crank has another pupil, too: Rambaud, the underwear salesman, whom Monsieur Médor still insists is a policeman! He's a nice chap and very good company. Since the attempted theft, he has frequented our little club and Robert has no more faithful supporter. He takes the place of Jules, who after the first flush of enthusiasm seems to have lost interest in the team's future.

Sitting in front of your foaming *stein* of German lager, try to picture the scene: the abandoned quarry looking a little like a miniature circus ring. In the middle a nice open, flat space. At one end a sort of tumulus or mound of earth from which the Crank directs operations, surrounded by his pupils. He has taken his stand up there as a safety measure: we have not yet all mastered the art of the *controlled* skid! Rambaud and I, keen though we are, are still just skidding and when Ferblantine and Rambaud's 404—he has sold his 2 CV to buy a more powerful, faster car—start cavorting about the track, it is best to stand aside . . . The treat is to see Robert drive! The Crank gives the signal and he's off. We have stuck a few pieces of wood in our skating rink so as to make a sort of slalom course. At the first turn he accelerates a little. Ferblantine gives a shudder on the slippery clay, shakes her rear like a wild horse stung by a gad-fly, and starts to skid. If the driver is too rough with her or loses his head, she'll go right round and start spinning like a top . . . But Robert is at the wheel. 'The whole art of controlling a skid,' the Crank says very seriously, 'can be reduced to a formula: you must strike a balance between the three forces acting on the vehicle: the force of gravity, centrifugal force and the pull of the engine.' It's simple! Ferblantine slides on all four wheels into a position in which she would cut at right angles across the curved path we have traced for her if she were running normally. With the aid of acceleration and wheel, Robert keeps the balance: he 'back-waters', as it were; that is to say, with a series of little tugs, he gently pulls the front wheels over to the left . . . to control his skid. Wonder of wonders! Ferblantine gracefully comes round the bend in a regular curve, sliding all the way.

This idyllic picture of a controlled skid only applies to Robert. It isn't quite so simple in Serge's case. He 'backwaters' perfectly, correcting the car's deviations very well, but he hasn't Robert's 'feel'. The latter corrects the car's deviations with almost imperceptible touches of the steering wheel practically before they occur. Serge sometimes spins right round. Rambaud practises with his 404 so as to gain really good control of her. He can more or less stop a skid and bring the car back onto its original path, but he is like me, he can't *use* a skid to turn faster. The Crank says that will come naturally when we overcome our fear of it. Personally, I'm in no hurry and I've got all the time I need: I'm still well under the legal age to get a driving licence . . .

Robert has just come into the room. He sends his love and apologies for not writing . . . He wants to go to bed—he says it's late . . . A future champion must not drink, smoke, or have late nights! So I'll have to leave you.

Be writing again. Cheerio!

Jean."

10

DRIVEN BY A CHILLY WIND, black clouds raced low on the horizon. The crowd of spectators and competitors in the 6th Brie Rally cursed this summer that began as badly as the spring had ended. This particular year the promoters, feeling like a callous joke, had chosen the little town of Tournan-en-Brie as the starting point for their rally. It was quite a choice: no one had ever seen such a tricky course, with its twists and turns and ups and downs through a maze of minor roads. Owners of large-engine cars had turned up all the same, but they pointed out that it was just a practice for more serious events. "It's a put-up job!" they all protested. "They want to discourage us. There isn't a single straight stretch in the whole course that would let us use our speed. It's all for the little cars!"

The "little cars" agreed modestly but did not succeed in hiding their jubilation. They began to express their hopes that this Saturday in June would see the little Dauphine beat the powerful Jaguar. These comments, caught by attentive ears, went straight to a corner of the market square of the little town where the preparations for the start were taking place. There, a little apart from the others, two somewhat intimidated young men found themselves hemmed in by a group of supporters. From time to time one of the rally veterans would point them out to one of his old friends and rivals.

"Did you notice? New boys!"

"I know. They've just joined the club. The president said that he had tried to dissuade them from chancing their luck on their own . . . Duquesnoy was looking for a co-driver . . . He could have taken one of them with him. But they wouldn't hear of it. These kids always think they know best . . ."

Then the veteran leaned towards his old rival and whispered in his ear:

"Apparently that's Bricard, Fangi's former mechanic, who tuned their Dauphine for them . . ."

The other's eyebrows shot up.

"Bricard! That's unfair!"

"That's what I think. What are we amateurs expected to do against professionals? Their car can do ninety!"

"Which is Bricard?"

"The bald chap over there, waving his arms in the air."

The Crank was indeed waving his arms about in a spectacular fashion. In fact his entire body was in motion. The garage owner could not contain himself for joy. Even the Twenty-four Hours at Le Mans had never given him such a feeling of satisfaction. Thc Brie Rally had brought out the entire staff of the Garage de l'Avenir, with the sole exception of Jules. In his place, Rambaud had brought a friend of his, another salesman, who was interested in the competition. The whole gang fussed round Ferblantine and edged through the crowd in the square to take a critical look at the other competitors' cars. Each time that Jean, Adèle, Rambaud or his friend Barbier came back to the coral Dauphine with a new tip, the Crank crowed with delight.

"What did I tell you? You've got a chance. You win a rally on paper. You glance at the rules and at the course and you know if you can hope to do anything. I saw it at once. You ought to get a place. And I'm not talking about the index. I'm talking about the general results. You can compete on equal terms with the big cars! And in the additional tests, there's no reason why you shouldn't distinguish yourselves!"

As Robert and Serge were smiling, the Crank immediately counteracted his optimistic comments by saying:

"You watch out! You won't come in first! There are two Giullietta s that will leave everyone else behind if their drivers aren't absolute duffers. If you end up in the first ten, you're not doing badly for a start—not badly at all!"

"All right! All right!" Robert protested. "We aren't thinking of carrying off the first prize today. We are still beginners."

Serge kept nervously arranging and rearranging his maps and notes. As the navigator, he was responsible for keeping the correct speed. He had not slept for two nights. He would shut his eyes, start to doze off and then wake with a start two minutes later, having dreamed he'd taken the wrong turning.

"Don't worry," Rambaud told him, "you have reconnoitered half the course; it will be fine. As for the part you have to cover after dark, don't forget your opponents are in the same situation . . . I bet that everyone will be penalized!"

Adèle Bricard agreed fully . . . She had her ears open and had been listening the whole time to what was being said. All the competitors were complaining about the difficulty of the course.

Even if Robert and Serge made a few tiny mistakes they wouldn't eliminate them . . .

From the middle of the square, a loud-speaker called on the crew of car No. 45 to get ready to start. Serge looked at a list.

"It will soon be us," he said in a toneless voice.

The cars were starting every three minutes. After No. 45, it would be the turn of 37, then 14, then 27, then 22.

Number 22 was Ferblantine of the Daroux-Rivois team.

The two youngsters got into the Dauphine. Robert grasped the wheel and gave his supporters a pallid smile. Serge once more checked his papers.

Jean looked at his watch. It was ten to ten.

"You have nearly a quarter of an hour ahead of you," he said.

"Let them relax a little," said the Crank, dragging the others away from the vehicle. "They must try to relax."

"Car No. 14 to the starting line, please", snapped the loud-speaker.

"What!" exclaimed Serge. "They've left one out!"

He looked at his list again. The loud-speaker had failed to call out No. 37. So they would start sooner than expected.

"Start up your engine," the Crank told Robert. "There must be a mistake, but you never know."

Adèle went off for information to the far side of the square, near the flag marking the start and where the officials were.

There was an uproar round the organizers. Some people were shouting, others were protesting. Adèle elbowed her way to the front. The cause of the incident was a simple one. Knowing that he was going to be told to be ready in a few seconds, the driver of car No. 37 had quickly glanced over his machine and discovered that his right front tyre was flat. He had asked for a few minutes grace to repair it. The other competitors were saying in no uncertain terms that 37 should start when its turn came or not start at all . . .

"How long do you need to repair it?" one of the stewards asked the competitor.

"About ten minutes."

The steward studied the list of starters.

"Ask your opponents. If they are willing to start earlier, you can leave after car No. 22."

"O.K.," said the owner of No. 27, who a few seconds earlier had been telling everybody that this business had thrown out his timetable. "I'll make a sporting gesture."

"I knew you'd cooperate," said the steward.

"All we want now is No. 22's agreement . . . "

Adèle took a step forward.

"No. 22 agrees," she said.

Her intervention provoked some surprise. Adèle Bricard hadn't the look of a woman rally driver. She explained and the judges noted No. 22's agreement.

The owner of No. 37 ran to his car. From a distance, Adèle saw him set to work with his co-driver.

"Are you ready, children?" Madame Bricard asked when she had returned to Ferblantine. "You're to start three minutes sooner than expected . . ."

"I'd rather," said Robert.

"Me too," agreed Serge. "This waiting is getting me down."

"I should move up to the starting point," the Crank advised them.

In first gear, Ferblantine moved slowly to the other end of the square, followed by her supporters.

"Car No. 22 to the starting-point . . ." intoned the loud-speaker.

The spectators, the competitors' friends and the competitors themselves, who were wandering about waiting for their turn, craned their necks. They wanted to get a look at the youngest entrants for the Brie Rally. Ferblantine, in her coral coat, looked as though she were flushed with excitement. Robert, himself, was scarlet. Serge, on the other hand, was as white as an aspirin. All these eyes intimidated them both.

"All right then!" the Crank called out to them. "We'll see you go by at Bombon! In any case we'll be at the end of the section at Villeneuve!"

"You're sure two sandwiches each is enough!" clacked Adèle, the anxious mother hen.

There were a few stifled laughs.

"I hope they're dry behind the ears!" someone said.

There were several other jokes in the same vein, but they were completely devoid of acrimony. They had to tease the babies a bit, but everyone agreed they looked a nice pair. After all, they were not lacking in nerve to jump straight into the deep end . . .

"When I started," one character said, "I went the first time with a friend who already had two years of competitions behind him, and I'm glad I did. You must make sure of other people's experience!"

"Experience!" another exclaimed. "The only experience worth anything is what you gain yourself!"

The stewards had completed the last formalities. The timekeeper's voice rose above the crowd.

"Thirty seconds more . . . twenty seconds . . . seven . . . six, five, four, three, two, one, ZERO! GO!"

A last smile for the Crank and his friends. A wave from Serge. With a roar, Ferblantine shot forward. They were off! The Crank had not had time to open his mouth for his last piece of advice: "Be careful!" For the last quarter of an hour he had been hanging on to himself; those two words had been burning his lips, and he did not dare. He felt absolutely ridiculous —almost like Madame Daroux saying cars are filthy inventions! But it did not stop him worrying.

"I hope they'll be careful," he said to Rambaud, who was standing near him. The salesman reassured him. You could trust Robert. The boy was no flibbertigibbet . . . Besides, he would be careful not to take risks. Had he not said, that very morning, that the one thing he wanted to do was to finish? He was not worried about the place he came in.

Car No. 37 was already coming up to the start, after changing a wheel and mending the puncture. No. 37 was a little low-slung Austin convertible.

"Thanks," said the driver as he passed Adèle.

His co-driver looked at the garage owner's wife and quickly turned his head.

"I'm sure I've seen that face somewhere," she thought. She prided herself on remembering faces. She looked at the man driving No. 37. He was wearing dark glasses and his back was towards her. One of the judges called him and he was obliged to turn his head. Adèle saw him in profile. She was right, she had seen him before. The Austin shot off . . .

"Come on," the Crank said to his wife. "We'll go and have a cup of coffee somewhere, then we'll drive slowly to Bombon."

"We've loads of time," said Jean Daroux. "Serge reckons they'll get there at eleven-thirty. It's under twenty miles away."

The Brie Rally consisted of two sections and two supplementary tests. The first section was to take the competitors from Tournan-en-Brie to Villeneuve-les-Bordes. As the crow flies, there were only just over thirty miles between the start and the finish. The organizers' genius for complicating matters had multiplied that distance by six. Before reaching port, Robert, Serge and their opponents would have to cover over 180 miles through a labyrinth of narrow roads. Once they reached Villeneuve-les-Bordes, the competitors would have to undergo a handling test and a speed test. Finally, when it got dark, they would have to take the road again to get back to Tournan, which they would reach after 120 miles of roads as tricky as those they had taken that morning . . . This formula: a high mileage over a small area gave supporters and friends the chance to post themselves at certain points on the course so as to see the competitors in action. After serious thought, the Crank had decided to wait and see Robert and Serge go by not far from the little village of Bombon. Then they were to meet up at Villeneuve-les-Bordes for lunch so as to be in position for the finish.

The little group therefore gravitated to a café where they forthwith argued the chances of Ferblantine and her two humble servants. Adèle was a little distracted, however: her mind was elsewhere. Suddenly she dropped the spoon with which she was chasing a lump of sugar round the cup.

"Got it!" she said. "I can't think why I didn't see it sooner."

"Eh!" said the Crank, bewildered.

"Eh!" said the others.

"Yes, one of the drivers of that Austin, car No. 37," Adele explained. "I recognized him. He came to the garage two or three days after the attack. He had a Simca Aronde."

"So?" said the Crank, who couldn't care less.

"That's all. I now understand why he turned his head when he saw me. I must say, he looked quite different the other day . . . He had such a reception that he didn't dare come back . . ."

"You see, Monsieur Rambaud," Auguste Bricard tried to continue, "the importance of modifying the cam-shaft is this . . ."

Rambaud was not listening to him. He was looking at Adèle, with knitted brows.

"You're sure you recognized him?" he asked.

"Quite sure. I never make a mistake."

Rambaud called the waitress and paid for the coffee.

"There's no hurry," protested the Crank, still thinking of his cam-shaft.

"I've just thought of something!" Rambaud said. "We aren't very far from Melun. I've a customer there. I'd like to pop over and see him. I'll meet you either at Bombon or at Villeneuve . . ."

"All right!" the garage owner said resignedly. "We'll get off, too. We might as well get a move on. You never know with Rosalie. She's stubborn as a mule!"

The rally had brought several hundred motorists to Tournan.

The Crank and Rambaud had only been able to find a parking space right outside the town, on the Coulommiers road . . . Rambaud and his friend Barbier strode off . . .

"Hey! Where's the fire!" Bricard protested, as he tried to keep up with them.

The salesman and his friend slowed down. Jean saw them glance at each other.

"What's up?" he asked Rambaud. "You look nervous."

The other smiled and reassured him. He was just in a hurry, that was all. He wanted to be done with his customer in Melun as soon as possible.

"But you're right," he said, "there's no need to gallop."

They were a hundred yards from the place where they had left their cars. The Crank's Rosalie was the nearest. The salesman's 404 was a little farther off, wedged between a van and an American car.

They were ten yards from Rosalie, when Jean Daroux gave a cry.

"Wow! The Crank won't like that!"

Bricard and his wife heard.

"What won't I like?" the garage owner growled, quickening his step. "Has yet another swine dented one of my wings?"

Rambaud, Barbier and Jean went up to the car. The two men, who had not previously noticed anything, saw what had caused Jean's exclamation. Rosalie's tyres were flat.

"Well!" they said.

They were so astonished that that was all they *could* say.

Rosalie had flats—in all four tyres. Some vandal had slashed them. The sight made the Crank utter a kind of roar, whilst Madame Bricard clasped both her hands to her heart as years ago she had seen the second leads do in the melodramas at the Théatre de l'Ambigu.

"The car!" shouted Rambaud.

The Crank, Adèle and Jean were stricken to see Barbier sprinting off in the direction of his friend's 404.

Rambaud, uncertain what to do, watched him go. Out of respect, no doubt, for the agony on the Crank's face, he stopped where he was. At that particular moment he wanted to show how much he sympathized with the garage owner.

"The rats!" spat out the Crank when he finally regained the use of his tongue.

At that same moment there was another cry. Jean,

the Bricards and Rambaud spun round in the direction in which the salesman's friend had disappeared.

. "It's Barbier!" cried Rambaud, who in his turn went off like a rocket.

A third cry went up to the heavens when he reached his car. The Bricards and Jean saw him running round the 404 and looking in all directions.

Finally he bent down and disappeared from sight.

"Something must have happened," Jean said.

All three dashed up.

Rambaud was bending over an inanimate body, lying on the ground just under the Peugeot's bonnet.

"He's been slugged," he said laconically.

Barbier's eyes were closed and his nostrils pinched.

The Crank had immediately seen, with his professional eye, what it was all about. Someone had started to undo the bolts in 404's front wheels.

"They were in the act of stealing the wheels when he got there," he said.

Rambaud nodded. It was easy to reconstruct the crime. The thief or thieves had attacked the car only a few minutes previously. Jean's exclamation had given warning of their party's arrival, and Barbier had been caught unawares.

"We must take him to a doctor," said the Crank. "If his skull's as hard as mine, he'll escape with a few stitches . . ."

Barbier sighed and opened his eyes. He groaned and put a feeble hand to his face.

"The brute," he groaned.

"How do you feel?" asked Rambaud anxiously.

"Tired." (Barbier managed a smile.) "My dear chap, I was caught like a kid . . . The fellow was hiding there . . ."

Barbier gestured towards the car parked next to the 404.

"I saw the wheels had been unbolted, so I bent down. I felt someone behind me. I turned round . . . Too late . . . My reflexes are too slow; it served me right . . ."

"I'm going to take you to a doctor," Rambaud said.

"There's no point. I'm feeling fine now."

"Don't talk rubbish!"

Barbier glanced furtively at the Bricards and Jean. They were standing there looking thoroughly embarrassed. Adèle, especially, had a disapproving look in her eye. Really, this man Rambaud! He didn't seem particularly upset to see his friend in this state.

"How are you going to get out of this jam?" Barbier murmured. "I think we've made a mistake. Things are moving too fast for my liking: it might be better . . ."

The salesman interrupted him, saying.

"Too late. It can't be helped—I can't go back now . . . don't worry. I'll park you with a doc, then I'm off."

Painfully, Barbier managed to struggle to his feet. Madame Bricard supported him while the three others hurriedly put back the nuts on the front wheels.

The Crank lifted the bonnet of the car and looked at the engine and the wiring.

"They haven't touched anything," he said. "She ought to go."

Rambaud switched on and started the engine.

Barbier heaved himself into the seat beside him.

"I don't know if I'll have time to meet you at Villeneuve," Rambaud said. "With all these incidents . . ."

The Crank flung up his arms.

"With all this I had almost forgotten our two champions," he exclaimed. "Bombon's out," he added. "By the time I've done the repairs . . . We'll try to make Villeneuve . . . If the kids don't find us there, they're going to worry . . . If you can meet us there, I'll buy you lunch!"

Rambaud promised to do his best and went off.

"Let's go and look at Rosalie," Bricard said when the 404 was out of sight. "I don't know if we're going to manage to do anything with those slashed tyres. There's a pal of mine who's a mechanic in these parts: he might be able to give us a hand."

The Crank had only just started to examine his car when he gave a howl of rage. He had lifted the bonnet and was staring in horror at the oil intake.

Jean Daroux and Adèle leaned over the engine.

"It's not possible!" groaned Jean. "Why have they done it?"

The vandal, not content with slashing the tyres, had smashed in the oil filter with a cold chisel and poured sand into the crank case. Rosalie was completely immobilized—useless. The Crank straightened up and turned round to his wife and the boy. Tears of rage and misery were rolling down his cheeks.

"There's n-nothing to be do-ne," he stammered. "It will all have to be dismantled. And there the kids are all alone . . . Someone hates us, Adèle. I'm hit over the head, we're robbed, Monsieur Rambaud's friend is slugged, too, our cars are sabotaged . . . WHY?"

"But we haven't any enemies," whispered Adèle, crushed by her husband's distress.

"Monsieur Médor claims it all started when we got Ferblantine," Jean said, half to himself. "I'm beginning to wonder if the old fool isn't right."

* * 11 * *

THEY HAD BEEN DRIVING for three hours. A hundred and eighty long minutes had gone by since they left Tournan-en-Brie. They felt terribly alone, cut off from the world, in their little brightly-painted metal hull.

Robert's hands held the wheel firmly but not too tightly. His feet danced their almost invisible dance: brake—clutch—accelerator. His right hand slipped almost furtively down to the gear lever. The engine screamed at full revs in second, roared in third and purred contentedly in top. Ferblantine glided along the macadam carpet.

"Hungry?"

"No . . . What about you?"

"Nor am I . . . Still, pass me a sandwich . . . We must eat; it's bad to live on one's nerves."

The second hand of the chronometer inexorably ticked away the seconds, and the minute hand, the minutes. There was a crackle of paper: Serge was shuffling his maps and notes.

"What's up?"

"Nothing. All's well: I was just checking. According to my landmarks, we're just about to cross a side road

. . . A hundred yards farther on there's a huge oak tree. You'll see a road on your right, the D 32."

"O.K. I'll be on the lookout. What a bore! It's starting to rain!"

The windscreen wiper buzzed away rhythmically while the rain fell like a curtain on the countryside . . . Ferblantine swung along the wet road . . . In front a cyclist, hampered by his raincoat, zigzagged along . . . Careful! A little lane leading to a house came out on the left-hand side of the road . . . The man would be going home. It was raining so he would turn without giving the smallest signal, without looking . . . Robert took his foot off the accelerator and braked gently. He had guessed right. The cyclist swung left, then saw the car, and his eyes rolled in terror as he realized how narrowly he had just escaped death . . . Robert shrugged his shoulders; Serge swore between gritted teeth. Driving is a matter of foresight. The experienced driver is never caught napping: he anticipates cyclists' and other motorists' reactions . . . It is a sort of sixth sense.

"Something has happened to the Crank and Rambaud . . . Why weren't they at Bombon?"

Serge didn't answer. He didn't know. He was worried. He couldn't understand it . . . Besides, there was the average speed to maintain, with this rain that was falling in buckets . . . At Bombon—what a name for a village!—they had strained their eyes to catch a glimpse of their little band of supporters. They had not been at the rendezvous . . . At one turn a crowd had collected. Robert had slowed down. Crawling past they had seen what it was: a car had missed the turning, doubtless sliding on the muddy surface, and had crashed into a wall. It was a Porsche with a huge white numeral on the side: No. 19, one of the competitors in the rally.

A villager had called out: "It's nothing!" In the middle of the crowd they had glimpsed two gesticulating figures who must have been the drivers. They had driven on and Robert had unconsciously raised his foot a little off the accelerator.

The picture of the Porsche rammed into the wall danced before his eyes . . . Several times they had passed opponents, recognizable from the numbers painted on the body and two plates attached one to each end of the vehicle, saying: RALLYE DE LA BRIE.

"I have a feeling quite a lot of people will have lost points by the time they get to Villeneuve-les-Bordes," Serge had commented.

He had not elaborated, but that meant: "We're doing all right . . ." On this particular course and in this filthy weather that prevented them from ever pushing up the speed, the smallest mistake was disastrous. If only the Crank and the others had been at the rendezvous, everything would have been perfect . . . Anyway, they would soon know. Every turn of the wheels brought them near the end of the section.

They passed two controls. At the second, one of the officials nodded and said: "By Jove! The kids are going well!"

When they went off again, they swelled with pride.

"I'm sure we aren't far behind the leaders," Serge exclaimed. "Did you hear what that character said? He ought to know how everyone's placed."

"We can't be doing badly," answered Robert, "but don't let's count our chickens . . . We haven't got there yet."

A steady drizzle fell from a leaden sky. Ferblantine sent fountains of muddy water spurting up on either side. They came to Le Châtelet-en-Brie. Only twelve miles to the end of the section. A mere nothing! The

213 ran due east. They passed Les Ecrennes and plunged into a forest between two walls of dark green foliage. It began to rain harder again. The road was deserted.

Robert thought aloud:

"It's not very nice weather, but at least we're left in peace. If it had been fine, the Parisians would have taken advantage of its being a Saturday to go out for a drive . . ."

They went over the Huit-Routes crossroad. It was a hundred yards farther on that they saw the motor cyclist. He was standing in the middle of the road, a forbidding sight in his black oilskin glittering in the rain, his helmet and his big motoring goggles.

"A speed cop!" said Serge.

"Where have you seen speed cops waving red flags?" Robert laughed, slowing down to stop.

In competitions, a red flag being waved means you must stop at once, which was what they were being ordered to do.

Ferblantine came to a standstill. Robert wound down his window. He noticed from the badge pinned to his oilskin that the man was a member of the Automobile Club.

"There's a detour," the motorcyclist said. "Take this forest track; it will bring you out to the D 67 and from there you can get back to 213."

"That's fantastic!" cried Serge.

The man made a gesture that implied it was nothing to do with him and waved his hand towards the track.

"Everyone says the same thing," he grumbled. "There has been an accident at the crossroads on the 56 . . ."

Serge and Robert exchanged a glance. They were thinking of the Crank and the others. The man reassured them. It was a tank wagon that had turned over and was lying across the road. He didn't want to go into any more details. He was dog-tired. His face was splashed with mud. And he had caught a cold in all this rain.

Robert changed into first, let his clutch in and started off down the forest track. It was motorable—at any rate, the first 200 yards you could see were motorable; then there was a turn . . .

"I have never been on a rally," Serge muttered, "but it's the first time I've heard anything like this. Only one single man to tell the competitors there's a detour . . . What *are* the officials doing?"

Robert was more fatalistic. He said nothing and stepped on the accelerator.

The track turned left then, a hundred yards farther on, turned right again into the heart of the forest of Villermoy.

Serge feverishly studied his map. The motorcyclist had been right. One thing was sure: they would come out onto the D 67.

"If we get there," Robert put in in a rather worried voice.

And indeed, after the second turning, the track became distinctly worse with quagmires everywhere. The rain, which had fallen almost without a break since dawn, had not helped matters. Ferblantine skidded along the ruts made by the timber carts. They pitched their way for another 300 yards. They were just coming up to a forester's lodge, with closed doors and shutters, when Robert stopped. Water had accumulated in a depression of the road. A pool, nearly twenty yards long, barred their path.

"Can't we get through?" Serge asked anxiously.

"It depends on the depth of the water. There's the danger of flooding the engine . . ."

They got out and looked perplexedly at the blackish pond. Robert picked up a dead branch and plunged it into the muddy water.

"It's six inches at the edge. It's a real quagmire. If we go in and get stuck, we'll be out of the rally for good!"

Nothing infuriated the tidy-minded Serge more than seeing a meticulously worked-out plan wrecked by some single incident. He resented this mishap as though it were a personal insult.

"There's no reason why we shouldn't get through it," he said. "It must have been foreseen! A rally isn't a cross-country race. Besides, if this pool were impassable, we wouldn't be the only ones here!"

Robert put a hand on his friend's arm.

"Look," he said.

He pointed to the continuation of the track on the other side of the pool.

There was no sign of tyre marks!

"Still they couldn't have jumped across," murmured Serge. He had automatically lowered his voice. The forest suddenly seemed hostile.

Only the drumming of the rain on the leaves broke the silence. Damp rose from the ground with the faintly nauseating smell of humus. Sitting in the middle of a tiny clearing, the forester's lodge seemed to be watching the two boys through half-closed eyes.

"It's sinister here," Robert said, shaking himself. "We must go back on our tracks."

This suggestion was fiercely opposed by Serge.

"We'd be eliminated! A course is a course! Besides, the others have found the answer."

"Look! Right beyond the pool, there *are* wheel marks . . ."

It was true: fifty yards the other side of the water's edge there were a number of ruts in the track.

"Let's go!"

They both took off their shoes and, keeping close to the bank, waded through the mud to the far side of the obstacle.

Serge had been right. A car *had* gone that way! Its driver had discovered a sort of path which went round the obstacle by forcing its way through the dense undergrowth on the side of the track.

Serge cursed. His conception of rallies had been turned upside down! A single car had crossed the obstacle: the others, therefore, had failed to meet the organizers' demands. Were they out of the rally? If not, was it better to avoid the obstacle and find another road—and risk being heavily penalized?

"Dash it, they can't eliminate everybody," he expostulated to Robert. "We're bound to be placed!"

Then another possibility struck him.

"Yes . . . but then a car has got by. One. The organizers have most likely placed a control on the 67. If we get there too, we're certain to be second."

The thought of a practically certain second place—even the first, for you never knew—decided the two friends.

"The beginning of the path our predecessor took must be before the last turning," said Robert. "You follow the path. I'm going to go backwards in reverse and we'll meet . . ."

Serge put his shoes on again. Robert bravely splashed back through the pool. Scratched by brambles and whipped in the face by branches, Ferblantine's navigator retraced the embryonic path that their lucky rival had opened up to motor traffic.

The car had literally breached the undergrowth like a projectile. Serge winced: poor Ferblantine, she *would* be in a state when she came out of there! He advanced some thirty paces and came out in a little clearing. Piles of logs, neatly arranged, bordered the path, which at this point looked like a perfectly respectable track.

Suddenly Serge gave a start.

A tree barred his way. Admittedly, it was no centuries-old oak, only a young elm with a trunk some five inches in diameter.

"That's the end!" he exclaimed.

Serge was not stupid. He reflected that the tree could not have fallen down between the passing of the other competitor's car and their arrival in the area . . . They had not noticed a tornado in the district . . . The man in the black oilskins would have made *some* mention of it—tired though he might be. While he considered, he examined the cause of the trouble. The elm owed its horizontal position to the patient work of a wood cutter. He also noticed that the wheel marks passed under the felled tree.

The deduction was simple, particularly as the earth and grass all round it were trodden and trampled . . . The competitors who had preceded them had used the tree like a level crossing they might have found closed: they had shut it again behind them. They had put the tree back in position. It was not a very sporting gesture, but Serge did not waste time worrying about that. As loudly as he could, he called Robert to his aid.

Two minutes later the latter arrived on the double. From Serge's first words, he understood what had happened.

"Let's get cracking!" he said, with a symbolic gesture of rolling up his sleeves.

Splashing about in the mud, pulling and pushing and puffing and blowing, the two of them set to work in the rain, which was still driving down. They pushed and pulled and panted in a sort of cold rage against the elements and the seconds and minutes that were ticking away. Silently, unwillingly, the elm began to shift . . .

Suddenly there was a noise. Not one of those extraordinary noises that makes the hair of imaginative people stand on end: just an ordinary, familiar noise that in other circumstances would have been reassuring: a sneeze!

In some situations, a common or garden sneeze can stop your heart beat. Imagine a hermit, alone in his wilderness, hearing this sonorous human sound only a few feet away from him! The muttering of an earthquake would surprise him less. Robert and Serge were in the position of such a hermit. There was someone behind one of the piles of logs. They were being watched. They thought they were all by themselves right in the heart of the huge forest—and quite close to them someone had sneezed!

They looked at each other uncomfortably.

"Did you hear that?" Robert whispered.

"Yes, someone's there all right," said Serge.

"Anyone there?" he then shouted to the forest. But the trees just muttered under the lashing rain. A branch cracked. A bird chirped at the far end of the little clearing.

"Oh well," said Robert, "it must have been a wood cutter or someone. Let's get this finished. We're wasting time."

He bent down to seize hold of the elm again. He glanced mechanically in the direction of the piles of logs in the vague hope of seeing the man with the cold. Serge, who was opposite him, saw his mouth become round with surprise and his features grow taut.

"Ah-h-h!" Robert exhaled like an inner tube letting the air out.

His navigator was shaken by his look of bewilderment and asked anxiously:

"What's up?"

Robert pointed at a log pile some distance from the elm.

"I saw—at least I thought I saw Jules . . . Jules Langlois . . . from the garage."

"You're mad!" exclaimed Serge, turning to look himself.

"I don't know . . . I just saw his head . . . He was watching us . . ."

If it had been anyone but Robert, Serge would have become angry. But he knew his friend: he had never known him subject to hallucinations. At that moment a door slammed and they jumped.

But they had heard no car arrive. It hit them simultaneously: Someone was interfering with Ferblantine!

This was too much. For some minutes they seemed to have been living in a sort of hostile fog. There had been the man in a black oilskin on the road, the impassable track, the elm that had been moved and put back . . . and then Jules. What was he doing in the forest of Villermoy? Why didn't he come out into the open? Robert might have been mistaken—that was most likely—but there still remained the fact that *someone* was watching them . . . And now, who was touching their car? Insidiously the feeling of uneasiness that had taken hold of them was turning to panic.

"I've had enough," cried Serge, whose nerve was breaking. "Let's go back!"

"I've left the ignition key in!" Robert exclaimed. "Quick!" They plunged through the undergrowth that separated them from the forest track, so as to get there as soon as possible.

Robert shouted out for luck: "We're here! We're coming!"

As wet as water spaniels and out of breath, they

floundered in the brushwood, tearing their clothes.

They had gone barely ten yards when behind them, from the clearing, they heard "Cuck-oo! Cuck-oo! Cuck-oo!"

They thought they heard stifled exclamations from the direction of the track, metallic sounds and a thud . . . They didn't know . . . The smallest crack of a branch sounded like a gunshot in their ears and the call of the cuckoo turned into a hideous snigger . . . Panting for breath, they emerged onto the track.

Ferblantine was there still, but . . .

"They've pushed her into the pool!" cried Robert, trying to see if anyone was hiding in the surrounding bushes.

The coral Dauphine was in the water almost up to her hubcaps. The two boys went in after her—this time without worrying about their shoes.

"Look!" Robert exclaimed. "My door's not shut . . . there are muddy hand prints on the window!"

By now a real panic had seized them. They had only one thought in their heads: "We must get out of here as fast as possible!"

Robert got behind the wheel. The engine started on the first try, it had not been flooded.

"I'm going to reverse out," he said. "Help me."

Serge, arched over the bonnet, shoved, slid and fell on his knees in the filthy water. Ferblantine started to move. Just touching the accelerator, letting out the clutch a tiny fraction, Robert gently eased the Dauphine out of her critical position. The Crank would have been pleased with him. He had remembered and assimilated all his lessons: "If your car is stuck in loose ground, try to get her out without making the wheels spin. You must use your own holes, so if you get stuck going forward, you must go out backwards."

Robert put his wheel hard over with the object of turning right round. Gradually he was regaining confidence . . .With the wheel in his hands and his feet on the pedals, the reality of familiar gestures gave him reassurance. The panic that had shaken him a moment before was dying down. He had already half turned the vehicle when Serge cried out:

"A car!"

A car had just appeared at the end of the track, lurching along the ruts. It was still only a moving black dot, practically invisible behind the curtain of rain.

"We had a wonderful lead!" Serge laughed.

He was smiling. The nightmare was over for him, too. This car was a solid proof they had not lost their way. The forest suddenly seemed less hostile and the forester's lodge stopped looking at them with an enigmatic air. But a new problem had arisen. Other competitors were going to pass this way and tackle the pool—perhaps with success. And there they were, preparing to go back! Staring at the black dot, they wondered what to do.

"They've stopped," said Robert.

Narrowing their eyes to see better, they tried to work it out. As far as they could see at that distance, it was a low-slung sports car. Perhaps the team was in difficulties. Then, in the distance, the angry growl of a second engine broke the silence. Another vehicle was approaching and its driver was dragging it through the mud on the track by roaring his engine. It was still out of sight behind the bend.

"He isn't so hot!" was Robert's comment on the obviously inexperienced motorist trying to bash his way through. At the far end of the track, the black dot moved and turned into a thin line. Two silhouettes broke away from it and disappeared into the copse.

"What on earth are they doing?" said Serge. "You can't see a thing in this damned rain!"

The second car appeared round the bend and stopped behind the one blocking its path.

It gave a blast on its horn, then another.

At the end of the long tunnel of foliage, Robert and Serge watched a strange, incomprehensible ballet. They might have been looking at a badly adjusted TV set, for all the gesticulations and shouts meant to them.

The picture was distorted by the rain and the sound by the distance. A man had got out of the second car. Then the two black figures, which a minute previously had vanished among the trees, reappeared on the road.

"They look as though they're quarrelling", said Robert. "Perhaps we should go and see what's up."

"They must be trying to extricate the little car," Serge hazarded.

One of the figures detached himself from the others and made as though to come in the two boys' direction. He was waving his arms about.

They then heard a whistle and faint, apparently meaningless, words.

". . . mean business! . . . Do you hear . . . Clear off!"

"He's calling to us," Serge said. "Switch off, I can't hear what he's saying." And turning towards the pygmy figure jumping about 300 yards off, he shouted, stressing each syllable:

"What—is—the—mat-ter?"

The question was lost in the tall trees, drowned in the sheet of water hissing down from the sky.

"AT—CHOO!"

Robert and Serge looked at each other. Someone had sneezed right beside them in the undergrowth. Jules' double was still watching them!

Then twenty yards away, under the trees but on the other side of the track this time, near the forester's lodge, someone grunted. There was a sound of breaking branches.

"We must get on with it," a voice said distinctly. "I have had enough of playing hide-and-seek."

It was happening again: the forest was suddenly bristling with life, the trees were speaking. Once more, terror seized the two boys.

Now there was no doubt about it. There were definitely people walking through the undergrowth—and coming towards them.

"They must have flooded their engine," an invisible voice remarked.

"We'll have to rough them up a bit," answered a second voice.

They were quite close. Robert and Serge stared as though hypnotized at the brush.

Branches began to move.

"We'll have to rough them up a bit . . . we'll have to rough them up a bit . . ." The words hammered in their heads.

"They must have flooded their engine" . . . that meant them all right. But why "rough them up"?

"I'm scared!" groaned Serge, leaning up against Ferblantine.

All his ideas about rallies were in turmoil. No rule or report mentioned this sort of adventure. Competition was always pretty fierce, but he had never read of competitors being beaten up by their rivals. He was playing a part in a "B" film made in slow motion, that was the truth of it . . . Actions and words were enveloped by the sort of whitish liquid the sky was pouring over them . . .

In bewilderment he looked at the TV screen at the far end of the track. The pygmy had grown. It was now an ordinary man—a short one, admittedly, but a normal man. And he was speaking. They could hear him quite distinctly.

He was saying:

"Take care of the kids! Let's get it over with!"

The angry roar of Ferblantine's engine, restarted by Robert, made Serge jump. He looked wildly round him, as though he were waking from a nightmare; the man was a hundred yards closer; he had come lumbering down the muddy track with great awkward strides. It had only taken thirty seconds, perhaps a minute . . .

The appearance of the first car, then the second, the hooting and shouting.

Suddenly he saw them.

There were two of them emerging from the brush, parting the branches in their way with broad sweeping gestures. Two men enveloped in long black oilskins, with crash helmets and goggles. They were some fifteen yards from Ferblantine, trying to tear a way through the thick hedge of brambles that separated them from the track.

The lips of one of these black ghosts moved:

"Hey! You kids! Beat it!"

One of the men in black leaped clumsily into the brambles. Serge felt his arms being seized. He was swung round on his seat, feet trailing on the ground . . . The driver's door slammed.

"We must go!" Robert's voice was saying.

Ferblantine gave a growl, leaped forward as though into the wood, then swung right. The muddy water spurted up. The men in black were shouting and staggering about. A dirty hand was clawing at Serge's arm. They were trying to drag him from his seat. In his terror he grabbed the hand and twisted it. There was a howl of pain. The hand disappeared. Ferblantine pitched and tossed in the mud. Robert, crouched over the wheel, kept as close as he could to the fence round the forester's lodge . . .

Of course the ground would be harder there, Serge realized. Then he thought of his feet: he had to get them back inside the car or they would hit something!

"We're going through," Robert shouted . . .

Serge glimpsed one of the men in black, standing in the middle of the pool. When Ferblantine had, so to speak, shied, she had temporarily blinded him. He was struggling to take off his mud-covered goggles. The other one was leaning against the fence, looking as though he had been hurt. Serge growled with joy: it was the one who had tried to grab him.

Ferblantine swung sideways and for a second was lying across the path.

The pygmy had become a giant.

He was now quite near the house. He was shouting. A second man came running up behind him, then another. The men in black were shouting, too. Their hopes revived.

The injured man flung himself after the car; the motorcyclist in goggles, now he could see again, was preparing a fresh attack.

Serge would have heard perfectly if it had not been for this damned cotton wool in his ears!

"Catch them! You clumsy fools! Robert! What rotten luck! Serge! Run for it!"

That was all very clear. They didn't mean them any harm as they were warning them to fly. That voice . . . Rambaud must be among them. A real friend. And Jules! He'd want to know what he was up to playing hide-and-seek in the woodpile! . . . Now Ferblantine was dancing about again . . . like a ballerina in her coral tutu! Left . . . right . . . left! And that door banging! That damned Ferblantine, if she wasn't taking off! It wasn't safe flying in these conditions . . . Lucky that Robert knew his job . . .

"Look out! I'm falling!"

Serge's eyes closed. He had fainted.

✵ ✵ 12 ✵ ✵

ROBERT DAROUX DELICATELY WIPED his co-driver's face. There was a thin trickle of blood running from Serge's hair down one grimy cheek. Robert gently felt his friend's skull. There was a fine bump the size of a pigeon's egg. So that was where the blood was coming from . . .

He must have banged it on something, Robert thought. "I didn't see anyone strike him."

He remembered that, just a minute or two previously, at the crucial point of this unbelievable adventure, he had jerked him violently backwards to make him sit down. There had been a dull thud. Serge must have cracked his head on the roof—hence the bump—hence the blood.

Serge sighed and opened his eyes.

"Phew!" exclaimed Robert in relief. "You gave me a scare!"

His navigator said nothing, but looked all around him. Ferblantine was parked on the shoulder of a minor road, surrounded by trees.

"I don't know what came over me," Serge said at last.

He hesitated a second before continuing:

"I—er—didn't dream it . . . In the woods, there really were . . .!"

Robert smiled. He need not worry, he was not mad. The men in black and the shouting were no nightmare . . .

"I made a dash for it," he explained. "Somehow or other we got through the water. Then Ferblantine spun round . . . I didn't catch what those characters were saying, but I managed to right her and drove straight on . . ."

Serge had completely recovered his senses. He looked at his watch. It said seven minutes past three . . .

"We were in the wood for exactly twelve minutes," he remarked. "I noticed the time when the motorcyclist sent us off down the track . . . Where are we?"

According to Robert, they were on the 67, a little road running from the D. 12 to the village of Echouboulains, through Echou Wood. They were still off course, though . . . Driving at their fastest, it would still take them a good quarter of an hour to reach Villeneuve, where they should have been at three minutes to three . . .

"We must go on," said Serge. "The Crank and the others are waiting for us. Besides, perhaps the organizers will be able to explain to us what the recent little masquerade was all about . . ."

They moved off again. At the junction of the 213 and the 67, they looked in vain for signs of an accident to a lorry . . . The rain had stopped, but the sky was still as grey as ever. They saw nothing and nobody. The 213 ran straight through the forest. Behind them, right in the distance, they saw a vehicle travelling fast . . . A belated competitor perhaps.

At Villeneuve-les-Bordes, the organizers had their hands full. Robert and Serge had been among the last to start, so most of the competitors had already arrived. The officials were installed in a huge tent in the Place de l'Eglise, which had been turned into a car park. It was the scene of an indescribable uproar. Hooting horns and roaring engines, the cries and lamentations of teams telling their supporters of their incredible misfortunes. If the truth must be told, Ferblantine's arrival passed quite unnoticed. Robert and Serge made their way to the control tent through two hedges of uninterested spectators. The timekeeper calmly announced the time taken by Messieurs Daroux and Rivois, "Five hours, twenty-four minutes, twelve seconds . . ." The loud-speaker dutifully repeated, "No. 22: five hours, twenty-four minutes, twelve seconds . . ."

Robert and Serge plunged into this fairground atmosphere, looked round them in bewilderment, without even thinking of getting out of the car, switching off the engine, or going and parking.

"What does one do now?" Robert asked his friend.

The latter had been through all the manuals, all the rules, but there was one thing he did not know: what a competitor was supposed to do when he had completed a section of the course.

The president, seeing their embarrassment and wanting to clear the arrival lane, quietly advised them to go to the park. They would be called later for the driving test . . .

Robert, overcoming his natural timidity, braced himself to ask:

"We're not out of the running?"

The president smiled good-naturedly. You learned to expect anything from these youngsters. They were complete innocents. And he had advised the other boy, the co-driver, whom he had seen when they joined the club, to start by going with an old hand. And the kid . . . (What *was* his name now? Ah yes, the Daroux-Rivois team, so the co-driver was Rivois). Well, this Rivois kid had almost laughed in his face. He had been perfectly polite, but . . . And here they were, quaking like little boys caught stealing the jam, because they hadn't completed the section in the time laid down. They must, however, have realized that if it was as simple as that to maintain an average speed in such weather and over a course bristling with traps, there would be no point in competitions. Everyone would win, so why start?

The president glanced at the list of positions. There were still quite a lot of calculations to be made; he had to check with the controls, add and subtract and penalize . . . But years of experience enabled him to have a rough idea.

"Eliminated?" he said. "I don't think so . . . As a rough estimate, you should be about twenty-fifth in the general placing . . . Out of fifty-five starters, that's not bad, particularly for a beginner . . . As for the Index of Performance handicap, you've done pretty well. You are tenth or eleventh . . . The small cars have the edge today."

Robert and Serge beamed. They knew a rally was not a race, but . . . all that time lost in the wood! Perhaps this was the moment to mention their adventure. The president had a kind face . . .

Serge got out of the Dauphine, and Robert followed his example.

"You'd best go and park," the official said, slightly annoyed to see what little notice these youngsters took of his advice. "You'll be in the way of . . ."

"Well, you see," Serge began, "we want to lodge a complaint . . . A complaint or . . ."

He hesitated, trying to find a more accurate word than complaint . . .

Two stewards had pricked up their ears. They went up to the president. What complaint was this?

One of them tactfully told the boys that their complaint could only be looked into at the end of the last section.

"Actually," Robert persisted, "it's not so much a complaint as an explanation we'd like. We were up to schedule and everything was going very well when, just past the Huit-Routes crossroads, a motorcyclist in a black oilskin stopped us. He was waving a red flag and wearing an Automobile Club badge. He told us that the course had been changed because of an accident and that we had to cut through the woods."

The steward who had already intervened went purple in the face. He was one of those apoplectic characters who have a passion for organizing and ordering people about. That a young whippersnapper of Robert's age should calmly state that "his" organization was not faultless because a motorcyclist in a black oilskin dared disturb it sent him into a rage.

"You should know," he said in an icy voice, "that only marshals wearing an armband, like these gentlemen and myself, are authorized to interrupt in the running of the competition!"

And he added nastily:

"It is not my job to tell you what a rally entails. There are printed regulations. If you obey them you will never have any cause for complaint."

Robert was a mild person, but in the good sense of the word. He was reserved, rather. He thought that one could always learn from one's elders. So he was never dogmatic except about things he knew for a certain fact.

"I'm sorry," he said. "I'm not accusing the promotors of negligence! I'm simply telling you that an unknown motorcyclist led us into a trap!"

"And I caught a crack on the head in the bargain," added Serge.

A president is by definition elected by a majority, often unanimously, "to preside". He is not a man: he is a common ground for conflicting opinions to meet and, if possible, to be reconciled. The president of the Automobile Club was no exception to this rule. His job was to oil the wheels. He felt that the discussion was getting out of hand. Soon people would be saying things they didn't mean. He broke in:

"Let's be calm, my dear Larrieu," he said, turning to the apoplectic steward. "There has obviously been a misunderstanding. These young men must have been the victims of a practical joker—or a maniac. We will untangle this tale later on . . ."

The gentleman named Larrieu bit back his reply with a "you-can't-fool-me" look that meant: "I see them coming, these young wise guys. Making up fairy tales to try and get a higher placing."

A competitor ran up. Larrieu and the president were wanted . . .

"There now, lads!" the latter said to the two boys. "We don't want to over-dramatize things, do we? Let's calm down and accept our placing like good sportsmen! We'll have to talk about this motorcyclist another time . . ."

The two boys were gently shepherded back to their car.

"I give up!" Serge exploded, as soon as Robert had found a place in the competitors' car park and switched off his engine.

They had been taken for opportunists!

"If the same thing happened to one of those gentlemen running a Jag," Serge said bitterly, "you'd have seen some action! But if you're not one of the big boys you're told to keep calm! On no account tarnish the glitter of the occasion. *Our* organization is impeccable!"

"I agree that if the Crank had been here, they'd have listened to us all night," sighed Robert. "I wonder what has happened to him. He must have broken down for once . . . But Rambaud!"

Serge's fury evaporated. That was true: what *had* happened to Rambaud?

"You know," he said, "it sounds ridiculous, but a few seconds before I passed out I thought I recognized his voice. Absurd!"

Robert nodded. It was just what he thought. What would Rambaud be doing in the forest? . . .

"After all, you saw Jules!" Serge riposted with a laugh. "Why shouldn't I have heard Rambaud's voice? All the same," he went on in a more serious tone, "this is a fishy business. Who do you think those people were? Do you really think it was us they were after?"

Robert confessed that the whole affair was incomprehensible to him. Unless . . .

"Perhaps we misinterpreted their waving and shouting . . ." he said. "We were tired and on edge. I must admit that forest played on my nerves. It was when I thought I saw Jules I really got scared. Fear is like a distorting mirror; it makes things look quite different."

Serge protested. He agreed he had lost his nerve, but that didn't explain everything . . . Those men in black were plainly hostile. They had ordered them to abandon their car! He was sure *that* had happened and he had not dreamed it!

"Fair enough!" Robert agreed thoughtfully. "That was what made me decide to make a dash for it . . . The president may not be so far off the truth in thinking that the men we met were thieves on the prowl . . .

They must have supposed that the competitors had a certain sum of money on them in case of emergency. They thought up the business of changing the course so as to get to work without being disturbed . . . It was a pure fluke that we should be the victims."

Not far from where they stood, a loud-speaker stuck up in a tree started crackling and finally announced in nasal tones that competitors in the Brie Rally were reminded that the driving test was about to begin. The competitors were to leave at three-minute intervals in the same order as they started at Tournan. They would have to cover three miles over a special course . . . Every obstacle touched would mean a ten-second penalty for the clumsy driver . . . the stewards warned competitors to prepare to examine the course . . . the public were asked to keep well back and the marshals responsible for controlling the crowds were told to be especially vigilant . . .

Serge buried himself in the plan of the course which had been issued to each competitor.

"You see," he said, showing it to Robert, "we have three sharp corners of almost eighty . . . The fourth isn't bad, you've already taken it to get here . . . Then there are two straight stretches of between 1,500 to 1,800 yards with chicanes every hundred yards . . . So now, Robert my lad, you'll be able to show them what you can do!"

Robert began to laugh:

"I thought you wanted to give up?"

Serge grimaced.

"Since we've got this far, we might as well go on. All the same, this evening when we get to Tournan at the end of the third and last section, we'll raise our objection!"

All round them in the parking area, engines were beginning to growl and doors to slam . . .

"Let's go and check the course," Robert said. "Then we'll see if it's possible to 'phone through to Le Plessis. The Crank may have returned to the garage . . . provided that he hasn't had an accident."

They drove slowly out of the parking area and started on the course laid round Villeneuve-les-Bordes . . . Preceded by a police patrol car, the cars drove at a slow speed. It was a matter not of testing but of reconnoitering the chicanes. The promotors had not been stingy with these. At intervals bales of straw half blocked the road. The longest clear stretch was barely 300 yards in length.

"I'm not surprised the owners of the big cars are protesting," Robert exclaimed as he swerved between two rows of bales. "A powerful engine won't be any help here. What's more, the road's slippery: it won't take much to send one sliding into the scenery!"

Serge scanned the grey sky . . . It was threatening to rain again.

"We should be called to the start at roughly half-past six," he said. "Let's hope it isn't raining then!"

Taking a firm grip of his steering wheel, Robert made a mental note of each obstacle. At the corner by the Bordes farm, the course left the D. 213 for a narrower road, an ordinary metalled secondary one. A second right turn brought the competitors back to Villeneuve. There were only two chicanes on this stretch. Robert grimaced. Serge, who read his every thought, said anxiously:

"The big cars will have a whale of a time here! They can gain four or five seconds on us."

"Providing they don't go off the road! It's a nasty surface . . . We'd best take it carefully."

He swung Ferblantine smoothly past the two obstacles that the promoters had cunningly placed there, and they arrived back at Villeneuve. Instead of going to the parking area, Robert turned left and stopped a little farther off on an esplanade, where he managed to squeeze in between two other cars.

"There's a telephone, all right," he said, pointing to the Grand Café de Commerce, whose bright red facade appeared twenty yards ahead. "We'll go and ring Le Plessis."

Robert locked Ferblantine's doors. They entered the café, which was already filling up with many of the rally drivers and their friends. Steaming hot rum was selling fast. The Grand Café du Commerce had a telephone, but the booth was taken. The two boys booked the next turn and ordered hot drinks.

"I'm starting to get hungry," Serge said. "Those two sandwiches I ate on the road have reached my heels. All this excitement gives you an appetite!"

Through the open door, gusts of music, relayed by network of loud-speakers all over the village, were drowned by the noise inside the café. Between two rain showers, the break in the rally was beginning to look like a fair. Stalls had been set up in the village streets. Shrieking children rushed about, chasing cach other, while their mothers threatened them with dire punishment. Farm workers stood stiffly in their Sunday best, gazing for ages at the competitors' cars whose big numbers painted on the bodies gave them a heroic air. From time to time the music would stop and the nasal voice would ask the drivers to get ready.

"Thc phone is free," the café proprietor told Robert and Serge, as he put down two steaming cups in front of them. "I'll get your number . . ."

Then he disappeared into the back lounge, sweating like a pig and quite bewildered by his customers' contradictory orders.

"Monsieur Robert Daroux wanted at the control,"

blurted the loud-speakers. "Monsieur Robert Daroux wanted at the control . . ."

Robert started. They meant him!

"Perhaps it's the Crank or Rambaud," Serge said.

"I'm going!"

"What about the telephone?"

"You take it."

Robert shot out of the café. He automatically glanced in Ferblantine's direction—a pure motorist's reflex: a yellow D.S. 19 had parked just behind, so she was jammed in.

Robert started to run: it was quicker on foot. The control was in the Place de l'Eglise, at most a hundred yards away. When he got there he had to hunt for the announcer. He was "somewhere around", they said. He couldn't be far off, they had just seen him . . . Robert eventually found the man with the stewards, making preparations for the handling test.

"I'm Robert Daroux . . ."

"Oh yes?" His name obviously meant nothing to the announcer.

"I was asked to come to the control."

"Of course, that's right. I made the announcement. I don't really know what it was about . . . I don't know who it was looking for you."

"Could it have been a man about sixty and bald—or a fair chap with a crew-cut?"

The announcer knitted his brows in an effort to remember.

"No . . ." he said. "It wasn't one of the stewards, I'm sure of that. He wasn't bald or fair . . . A dark-haired man, I think . . . I believe he had a moustache . . . And he was wearing dark glasses. He can't have gone far. Have a look round . . ."

Robert searched in the vicinity of the control. As he squeezed his way past little knots of people, his ear caught a babble of "minutes", "seconds," "turns", "rotten weather", and "impossible course". But there was no sign of the man with the moustache and dark glasses. He was more disappointed than intrigued. He had been sure that the Crank or Rambaud had at last reached Villeneuve, that he would have some news of his friends and his brother. But perhaps Serge had got on to Le Plessis . . . He started to run back to the Grand Café du Commerce . . .

When he reached the esplanade, he saw Ferblantine. A figure was bending over the coral Dauphine's door. Serge? . . . It was not his friend's light tweed jacker . . . Anyway, he knew that he, Robert, had the keys.

Robert stood still and watched the figure from the other side of the esplanade. He must be just a curious bystander. Then Robert's heart missed a beat. Could he be seeing things? The man had opened the door! Robert dashed over.

It was a man of about thirty, dark and sunburned, wearing a soft leather jacket and dark grey terylene slacks. He looked as though he had walked out of a fashion magazine, with his silk scarf. With his legs still on the ground, he was calmly settling down in the driver's seat!

"What are you doing in my car?" Robert asked in an expressionless voice.

The fashion plate raised a pair of elegant eyebrows. He had regular features and dark eyes that shone half with amusement, half with vexation.

"Is this car yours?" was all he said. (The raised eyebrows silently added: "Really, how fantastic! I never would have *dreamt* . . . believe me, if I had *known* . . .!)

"It is mine. The doors were locked."

This was really too much. The man emerged from Ferblantine and said, wide-eyed:

"You see, I've friends taking part in the rally . . . They have a car exactly like yours. I've been looking for them since this morning. I was getting into their car—or rather into your car—to wait for them. It seemed the only certain way of finding them. As for the door, I can assure you that it was not locked."

He spoke quite calmly with complete self-assurance. What he said was perfectly straightforward. Why should he raise his voice?

He was a head taller than Robert. He looked down at him with a courteous, even a sympathetic expression. He suddenly started to chuckle quite naturally.

"What a fool I am," he said. "I owe you my thanks as well as my apologies."

A baffled Robert stared at him open-mouthed. He was certain he had locked all the doors. It did not look as though the lock had been forced . . . but he could not very well check with the man standing there . . . Besides, the chap did not seem to have a bad conscience . . . A car thief caught in the act would have behaved quite differently . . .

"Yes," he was saying, "if I had noted the number, I would have remembered . . . And you're No. 22, what's more! It was thanks to you I was able to start at all. I had a blow-out just as I was about to move off. A lady came up and told the stewards you wouldn't mind starting three minutes earlier than expected . . ."

With a smile that revealed a row of perfect teeth, he held out a sunburned and sportsmanlike hand to Robert.

"Fernand Jamain . . . You and your co-driver must be the two youngest competitors."

Robert took the outstretched hand. He blushed with confusion—but he was won over. Monsieur Jamain was already speaking with enthusiasm of Ferblantine. What a fascinating little car! Was it true that the famous Bricard had tuned her?

While they were talking, Monsieur Jamain lit a cigarette. Robert bent down to show him how Ferblantine had been underslung. The man made a signal in the direction of the Grand Café.

"I'm just telling my co-driver I'm coming," said the elegant motorist as Robert turned round to see whom he was signalling.

He saw a man of average height dressed as expensively as Jamain just going into the café. He seemed to be wearing dark glasses. He thought that his upper lip was adorned with a black moustache, but he could not be sure.

"I must go and rejoin my friend," he said. "I've asked them to get a telephone number and . . ."

But the other had not been listening. He took Robert's arm in a familiar fashion and gently drew him to the rear of Ferblantine. How had the Crank and Robert solved the problem of the cam-shaft, he wanted to know. It was a problem that had always interested him . . . he had once thought of buying a Dauphine Gordini . . . At the moment he had an Austin. Under a thousand c.c.'s, so they were rivals. Today he and his co-driver had had rotten luck: the car had gone off the road. It was a nasty little turn that didn't look anything at all. Luckily, they had come out all right. No damage . . .

He went on and on. He had the knack of asking unanswerable questions. And he was so nice . . .

An engine being raced in the street a few feet away made him jump.

He stood on tiptoe to look over the tops of the parked cars.

"It's my co-driver," he said. "He's growing impatient. I must fly."

He gave Robert a friendly pat on the shoulder, promised him that they would meet again soon, and strode off. Robert, somewhat dazed after Jamain's flow of words, went off towards the café. Before he went inside, he turned round and saw in the distance Jamain sliding in next to his colleague. He had been right just now; the latter *was* wearing glasses and a moustache.

"Perhaps it was he who got the control to ask for me," he thought. "I expect he wanted to thank me for giving up my place at the start."

Serge was not in the café. On the counter Robert saw two cups of Viandox and a half-eaten sandwich. He beckoned to the proprietor.

"I asked for a call to Le Plessis," he explained. "Did my friend take it?"

The man made a superhuman effort to remember. He was becoming more and more swamped with work.

"Le Plessis . . .? I remember! Your friend did get through . . . Five minutes ago, at the outside."

He ducked under his counter to see if the indicator showed that the call-box line was still engaged.

"He's still talking . . . The box is at the rear: you go through the backroom, then through the kitchen and down a corridor. You can't miss . . ."

He had other things to worry about. Without even finishing his sentence he dashed to the percolator . . .

Robert crossed the back room, which was occupied by a broken billiard table and crates of beer bottles, penetrated into another room, which certainly was not the kitchen, but finally found the latter where an old lady was shelling peas. He opened a door which belonged to a cupboard and not the expected corridor.

"If you want the Gents," the old lady said amiably, "it's the other door. You go across the yard and . . ."

"I'm looking for the telephone . . ."

"It's engaged . . ."

"I know. I'm looking for a friend."

"That's all right then. Well, if you cross the yard you'll find a corridor . . . My son-in-law put a telephone there . . . His room is just above it, you see. It's better than having to run all the way to the café each time . . . Besides, it's nice for the customers, too. You don't always want people to overhear what you're saying, do you?"

Robert beat a strategic retreat. Once he had escaped from the chatter of the old lady with the peas, he set his course for the telephone booth.

The corridor *was* the booth.

The telephone was attached to the wall.

The receiver was off the hook and swinging lazily to and fro.

No sign of Serge.

A gargling sound was coming from the instrument. Robert put the receiver to his ear. A vexed female voice asked nasally: "Hello, Villeneuve, have you finished? Villeneuve, are you still holding?"

"Hello!" said Robert.

Modern life has so conditioned us. Certain objects start off certain reactions. A red light makes you stop or start—according to whether you are a motorist or a pedestrian. On the telephone you say, "Hello!" So Robert, a child of the twentieth century, said, "Hello!" This simple word let loose a torrent at the other end of the line.

"Hello, Villeneuve? Have you gone to sleep? Replace your receiver!"

"Someone had forgotten to," Robert tried to explain.

"Well, replace it now, please! You're no longer connected!"

"Isn't Le Plessis answering?"

"Le Plessis has hung up. Now I can't waste any more time, sir!"

Robert gave up, intimidated by the operator's peremptory tone. Serge might have looked what he was doing! He left everything in a mess and he, Robert, was the one who got the curses! Anyway, where had he gone? He had not seen him either in the café or out on the esplanade . . . He looked in vain in the deserted lavatories. He stood for a moment in the middle of the yard, utterly perplexed. Yet another mystery! The lady of the peas had been quite definite: there was someone on the phone. It could only have been Serge. Robert suddenly noticed a half-open gate on the far side of the yard. Who knows? He thought . . . and went to have a look. The gate opened into a lane running along the backs of the houses; beyond lay the open country and, half-hidden by a clump of elders, you could see the road. So it was possible to leave the café other than by the official entrance on the esplanade. But it was not like Serge to take off like like that without paying for the drinks . . .

Suddenly Robert's eye caught something glittering in the grass at his feet. He bent down and picked it up. It was a gold-plated ball-point pen.

"B—but," he stammered aloud, "I must be dreaming: it's not possible . . ."

There was no doubt about it though. He recognized that scratch near the clip. It was Serge's pen, all right.

He looked wildly round him . . . There was no other sign of his friend having passed that way. The grass near the gate had been trampled down but that was all . . .

Robert shivered. He felt an invisible hand clutch him by the throat. Once more, fear rose up inside him.

13

WITH HIS EYES GLUED to the starter, Robert Daroux sat waiting. The man's hand was raised. "Four . . . Three . . .Two . . . One . . .ZERO!"

He let out his clutch and pressed on the accelerator. Ferblantine shot forward with a fierce roar of her engine. Decelerate . . . clutch in . . . into second . . . clutch out . . . accelerate . . . Within the count of nine, the speedometer was nearly up to forty . . . The car went into the first turn. The easiest, Serge had said, "Watch it now! The first lot of chicanes are next. That was a mite too fast!" It seemed to Robert as though the four bales of straw were going to fly through his windscreen. With squealing tyres, Ferblantine skidded, slid between the two obstacles and shot off like an arrow.

In the crowd, people had cried out instinctively. Others had shut their eyes. So as not to see "it" happen.

"He didn't touch 'em!" someone exclaimed. They feverishly consulted the list of entrants. No. 22: DAROUX-RIVOIS . . .

"If he goes on like this, he'll do better than Roncier's Alfa," a connoisseur remarked.

Robert had taken the wheel as though in a dream. For an hour he had been moving through a kind of mist. What sort of a world was it? Was it possible that these faces, these objects that surrounded him should conceal some menace? And if they did . . . WHY? . . .

"Come, now!" he said to himself. "I'm not dreaming. I know Serge. He's not the type to vanish into thin air. People with a gift like that either tell their friends or betray themselves some time or other. So what? There must have been some ridiculous misunderstanding, as there had been in the forest. The old pea-sheller hadn't noticed him return . . . He had gone out of the café . . . Perhaps he had seen him talking to Jamain, the chap with the Austin. There! It was quite simple. Robert had paid for what they had had and for the telephone call. Ferblantine was still on the esplanade. That almost surprised him. After the Crank, Rambaud and Serge, why not Ferblantine? The series of disappearances would have been complete. However, he had recovered his car and reported to the control . . . Serge might have been looking for him . . . He had seen the president. He was in excellent form. Robert had been careful not to mention the motorcyclists in black oilskins . . . The one thing he wanted to avoid was any more trouble. Blue sky was appearing and the roads would dry . . . "Well, Daroux, fit? A bit rested? Don't forget, it'll soon be your turn . . . Don't miss it . . . I'm counting on you to do us proud. For the last two years the Marne Car Club has beaten us in the classification by clubs." The president was having himself a ball!

"I'm looking for my co-driver, Serge Rivois . . ."

"Haven't seen him. He must still be hanging around over there."

The president gave a jovial laugh that meant, "You're having bad luck today"—and a wink to show he had not forgotten the business about the motor-cyclist.

"Don't worry, Daroux," he went on, "you've until nine this evening to find him. You don't need a navigator for the driving test!"

What could he say? How could he explain? Serge should have been at the telephone, and he was not there. He had found his pen in the grass, near an empty lane . . . The man would laugh in his face. "Come, come, my boy," he'd say, "one wild story a day is quite enough!"

He had not pressed the matter: it was the announcer who had offered to use his microphone.

"Have you lost your co-driver?" he asked. "It's incredible! Villeneuve is a little one-horse place and yet everyone gets lost in it! You're at least the fourth in the same trouble . . ."

The loud-speakers had bruited Serge Rivois' name to the four corners of the village and informed him that Robert Daroux was waiting for him at the control.

After waiting for a quarter of an hour, Robert had left. He was wasting his time. He had driven Fer-blantine round the village just in case. But it had been in vain.

Suddenly an idea had come to him.

"According to the girl at the exchange, Serge got on to Le Plessis. So there was someone at the garage. The Crank must have had to return. Perhaps he told him something. Unless it wasn't the Crank . . .

Admittedly he could not really understand how Serge, even if he *had* thought he was wanted back immediately, could have disappeared without a word. But it seemed to him that he had had a good idea, an excellent one, in fact. He cursed himself for not thinking of it earlier. He went back to the Grand Café du Commerce, only to hear the loud-speakers warn the owners of car No. 27 to get ready. No. 27 was the car starting just ahead of him. He had no time to phone! He *had* to continue the rally.

After the driving test he would call Le Plessis . . . By nine o'clock, the time for the start of the third and final section, covered in the dark, he would have found Serge. There was lots of time to withdraw officially between now and then.

Sadly he made his way to the start. For years he had dreamed of the day of his first event. And these last few weeks, which had been so hectic for all of them! It should have been a culmination . . . And then he was all alone, surrounded by unknown faces, among people who couldn't care less . . .

"But I just must do something for the Crank," he said to himself. "Even supposing I have to retire, if I clock up a good time he'll be pleased."

He was so worried he had lost interest in the rally. He learned that the best time had been made by Roncier in Giulietta: four minutes, nineteen point three seconds!

This shattered him. An average speed of nearly forty-four m.p.h. on a course like that! This man Roncier was a champion!

"No. 22 to the start," announced the loud-speakers.

Robert quickly took up his position . . . They signalled to him to stop and wait . . . He glanced round him and saw the president and all the stewards. His pulse was racing . . . 4′19.3 . . . 4′19.3 . . . 4′19.3.

His hands tightened on the steering wheel.

"Go!"

One obstacle . . . two obstacles . . . the 300-yard straight, the only real straight in the course. Ferblantine went like a bullet.

"I must hang on! I'm scared and I know it. People who claim they don't know fear are either lions or clods . . . Even the champions are scared. Fangio, the great Fangio, was scared when he raced: the Crank often repeated that to me. One day Fangio had said to the Crank: "On one of the scales of the balance, there's that beast with its claws out, that squats in one's inmost self, tearing at one, body and soul . . . On the other scale there is the sum total of experience, complete knowledge of the road-holding qualities of the car you are driving. You must know exactly how far you can go—the calculated risk. Beyond that there's the love of the game . . . the love of the game and death . . ." More chicanes! Now's the chance for the small cars. You've got to be in the best possible position to tackle them . . . Why do they talk about "negotiating a bend"? "To negotiate" is a verb that implies a careful approach—a discussion . . . You don't negotiate with centrifugal force, speed and the grip of your wheels. You tame them, you bend them to your will. Between an unsuccessful negotiation and a turn there's a great gulf—or rather a ditch, *the ditch* . . . The trajectory you have to follow in a series of turns is the one that allows you to take the last turn at the highest speed.

Roncier knows that theory . . . 4 minutes 19.3 seconds . . . I'll never make it . . . Here comes another . . . Gently, Robert, don't get rattled . . . don't risk a penalty . . . Hand over . . . Watch that bend: there are chicanes just around the corner . . . Hard over! Like a pink streak of lightning, Ferblantine crossed the finish line and came to a standstill on the service track. Spectators and competitors looked at their stopwatches . . . There was a sort of moan from the crowd.

"I make it 4′20″ exactly!"

"4′18.9″."

"4′19″ and a fraction."

The loud-speakers crackled, then announced in a nasal voice:

"Car No. 22: four minutes and nineteen point one seconds!"

There was applause and exclamations.

At the end of the road the coral Dauphine was turning round and coming slowly back to the park. To everyone's astonishment, the president left the control and ran as fast as his little legs would carry him towards the car.

"Bravo, Daroux! Bravo!" he barked.

Robert, hearing his name, pulled up.

"I knew it my boy!" cried the president when he had got his breath back.

Robert had heard the adenoidal voice of the loud-speaker but had been unable to make out the words.

"Was I under five minutes?" he asked.

.."4′19.1″!" the other exclaimed. "You just beat Roncier and his Alfa by a fifth of a second!"

Robert shook with delight. He thought he had done a good time, but to beat Roncier!

"It was beautiful . . . just beautiful!" the president repeated. "You took some chances, but they paid off."

Robert's face, which had lit up with a smile at the good news, grew serious again. He tried to remember his actions and relive the past four minutes.

"No," he said simply, "it was all right, I just kept both pans of the scale equal . . ."

And as the other looked at him blankly, he added sadly:

"It's one of my trainer's, Monsieur Bricard's, expressions. I do wish he had been here!"

❋ ❋ 14 ❋ ❋

FOUR MINUTES AND NINETEEN point one seconds had been sufficient for Robert Daroux to pass from complete obscurity to relative fame. After the president, the stewards and the committee of the Automobile Club wanted to congratulate him. Roncier himself, the great Roncier, winner of the previous year's Tour de France Automobile and loser on the Villeneuve course, shook his hand. He wanted to meet the future champion. It was enough to turn the head of a boy of nineteen. Robert stayed very quiet. In any other circumstances, he'd have welcomed it all, the compliments, the smiles . . . Too many black clouds had overshadowed the day: the absence of his friends, the disappearance of Serge . . . He hurried off. He wanted to phone Le Plessis. It seemed as though Serge had got through, so the Bricards must be at home. He would find out what had happened to the Crank and ask his advice.

He was just entering the Grand Café du Commerce when he heard someone call his name. He turned round to find Fernand Jamain, the elegant man of the Austin and his co-driver with the moustache and black glasses. Jamain looked delighted. He gave Robert a friendly slap on the back.

"Fantastic!" he said. "That was a superb performance. Imagine knocking two tenths of a second off Roncier's time! Terrific!"

Then Jamain introduced his companion:

"This is my co-driver, Boudier."

Robert shook hands with him and asked politely what time they had made.

"Bah!" exclaimed Boudier. "Fernand persuaded me that I would be happier than him on that course and I was fool enough to believe him. The best I could do was 4′32″—*and* I knocked over a chicane."

They went on chatting for a moment. Jamain was sure that after his recent triumph Robert could not be far off first place in the "under 1,000 c.c." class.

"He's right," agreed Boudier. "We all had eyes bigger than our bellies. The reliability course seemed to be made for the small cars . . . Everyone was thinking of the general placing. And everyone rushed off round the course at top speed so as not to lose their lead to more powerful cars. The result was penalties galore. Chicanes were flying in all directions!"

While talking they made their way into the café. Jamain and his friend dragged Robert to a table at the back. The latter protested mildly. He had only come in to telephone . . .

"You'd better go and ask them for your number," Boudier advised him. "They always take a long time to get through."

The proprietor took their order and made a note of the number Robert wanted.

"By the way," he said, recognizing the young man, "did you find your pal?"

"Oh . . . er!" Robert stammered in embarrassment.

He did not want to discuss Serge's disappearance with the other two. How could he explain what was inexplicable? They would laugh at him. It seemed to him that the only thing to do at this juncture was to confide his troubles to the Crank.

But Jamain asked the inevitable question:

"Have you lost your co-driver?"

Robert smiled awkwardly.

"It's not serious. We'll find each other again before the start of the night section . . . the village isn't that big!"

The two men agreed politely. Obviously they were not particularly interested. They chattered of this and that for a moment or two; then suddenly Jamain, who could see the esplanade from where he was sitting, said:

"This friend of yours—isn't he a boy of about your height with dark hair, wearing a light tweed jacket?"

"That's right," Robert answered. "Why?"

"Well, a boy like that has just gone by. It could have been your friend. I'm not sure, mind, I only saw him this morning at Tournan, with you . . ."

Robert jumped up from his chair, followed by Jamain. Boudier remained seated.

He slipped through the knot of drinkers standing at the bar and reached the door. He could not see that familiar figure . . . He looked left: no Serge . . . He looked right . . .

On one of the panels of the wide-open double door there hung an advertisment-baromcter with a little mirror on it. In this mirror he caught sight of the miniature reflection of Boudier, who was leaning over the table they had been sitting at and pouring something into Robert's glass . . .

"Was it him?" asked Jamain, moving nearer.

Robert still kept his eye on the mirror. Boudier,

with a satisfied look on his face, had regained a more natural position.

"I don't know," Robert answered in a weak voice. He did not dare look at Jamain. His heart was pounding. He had seen it clearly enough: it was into his glass that Boudier had poured something. There was no possibility of his having made a mistake. He tried painfully to find a reason for him to do something so utterly incomprehensible.

"I think I saw someone turn down that street on the right," he went on. "I'll go and have a look . . . There's a chance . . ."

Jamain shrugged his shoulders and turned to go back to the table. Robert went out of the café. He felt his legs giving under him . . . He walked like an automaton to the end of the esplanade as he had said he was going to. He had to think, to work it out. What did they want with him? . . . Boudier had poured something into his glass . . . deliberately. First of all, what could the potion be? Stories of sportsmen drugged or poisoned by their rivals flashed across his mind. It was not that. Boudier did not want to stop him winning . . . Incidentally, hadn't he seen this Boudier character somewhere before? Where could it have been? That round face . . . The glasses and the moustache put him off. Suddenly he got it. Oh, he would not have sworn to it on oath, but he was pretty certain: Boudier was the man in the Aronde who had come to the garage just after the attack on the Crank; the one Adèle Bricard had surprised ferreting around in the junk . . . A man answering his description had had him called to the control just before Serge vanished. He was still floundering about in the dark. The events of this fantastic day still struck him as incomprehensible. But he thought he saw a faint glimmer of light in the darkness . . . Of course he *could* be the victim of a kind of hallucination. There was only one way to find out: to let himself float with the tide like a cork . . . to go on being fate's plaything . . .

He went back into the café, hoping that the others would not notice his state of nerves. He was afraid he would prove a rotten actor.

"Where were you?" the proprietor called out. "I got your number."

Robert bit his lip. He had forgotten the Crank. He apologized and asked the man to get it again.

"Wasn't it your friend?" Boudier asked anxiously when he had sat down.

"No. I went to the end of the street . . . It was a mistake."

Robert glanced cautiously at the table. The three glasses were half full. His and Jamain's were close together.

"I must try to be as natural as possible," he thought.

He tried to remember how he behaved when he was "natural". He wasn't quite sure.

"You look worried," said Jamain.

"I'm getting a little anxious about my friend . . ."

"There's no need," said Boudier. "He can't be far. Perhaps he's met a girl?"

The other two laughed. Robert followed suit as best he could.

He would have to drink his half glass of mineral water. He was scared. Suppose it *were* poison? But he had decided to be a cork, drifting with the tide of events. And the tide was these two men at the same table . . . He lifted the glass to his lips and drank half a teaspoonful. He thought that Jamain and Boudier seemed to be following his movements with passionate interest.

"Good Lord, they want to make sure that I drain the glass."

He put it down. The mineral water had no peculiar taste. Suddenly he felt a fool. He must be going crazy or something; he must have dreamed it. He was seeing everything through a distorting mirror!

"I'm out of cigarettes," Boudier remarked, getting up and going to the bar. At that second Jamain turned round after him and asked his friend to get him a pack of Camels.

For three seconds Jamain took his attention off Robert.

"If my drink is really drugged," thought the latter, "I'll see its effects without suffering from them."

He was still holding his glass, which was resting on the table next to Jamain's. He let go of it, grabbed the other and emptied it in a draught.

Jamain saw nothing.

Boudier came back. Seeing the empty glass in Robert's hand, he decided not to sit down again.

"I'm just going up to the control," he said.

"O.K.," answered Jamain with a knowing look.

He too had just noticed that Robert had drunk.

Robert had made the substitution without realizing that he had thereby ceased to be a cork. What should he do now he was supposed to have drunk his drugged drink? The sight of the glass had quite obviously decided Boudier to go off. Were they waiting for him to collapse on the spot as though pole-axed? Or to fall asleep in an hour? Or to start dancing a jig?

Boudier went out.

On the off-chance, Robert stammered:

"That's f-funny. I-I don't feel too good . . ."

A flicker of astonishment passed across Jamain's face.

"He looks surprised," Robert thought to himself. "I must have blundered. The stuff isn't expected to work so fast . . ."

Luckily the telephone rang and caused a diversion. Le Plessis was on the line.

Robert dashed to the phone. As he left the room he saw Jamain finish his drink and get up . . .

When the proprietor of the Grand Café du Commerce had announced that Le Plessis was on the line, he was just using a conventional phrase. In actual fact, the Crank was fighting his way along that line through the shrill cries and recriminations of two young ladies of the telephone service.

He said, "Hello." Robert said, "Hello"; the Crank said, "Hello" again . . . and again.

"It's ME, Monsieur Bricard," Robert shouted.

He had cried out for the benefit of all—and for a dry, sunburned hand that had calmly come down on the hook. He was cut off!

"It's a waste of time," Jamain said peaceably. "I've decided to ask you to dinner. We're just leaving."

He was a head taller than Robert and stood behind him with one hand on the telephone and the other on his, Robert's, shoulder.

"But I . . ." The boy was completely at a loss.

He did not dare rebel, although the whole proceeding struck him as being high-handed in the extreme!

"Be good! I'm sure you must be feeling very tired," Jamain went on with a hint of mockery in his voice.

"So!" He thought the drug was beginning to take effect! Robert, who after careful consideration was about to become extremely angry, suddenly relaxed. He had been about to forget he was a cork . . .

"I am a bit sleepy," he mumbled.

"Come."

The other took his arm, firmly but not unkindly. They crossed the yard and went out the back way. The Austin was parked beside the wall.

"I'm beginning to understand how Serge disappeared," Robert thought. "They carted him out through this gate; that was how he dropped his pen in the grass . . . Yet it couldn't have been Jamain or Boudier who kidnapped him. That was a physical impossibility . . ."

One thing was certain: the drug was supposed to put him to sleep. He climbed into the Austin with difficulty, like someone on the verge of collapse . . . Jamain took the wheel, drove off along the little road skirting the village and came out onto the D. 201 highway. Robert's eyes were closed and he appeared to be half-unconscious. He heard the driver yawn and mutter:

"This idiot's sleepiness is catching."

He had forgotten! Jamain had drunk the glass destined for him! He half-opened one eye . . . They were on a metalled road. There was a car behind the Austin . . . another small one . . . It hooted . . . He caught a glimpse of Jamain's arm waving it on . . . the car passed them. This time he nearly gave himself away. They had been overtaken by Ferblantine! And with Boudier at the wheel! He was driving fast . . . The Austin, on the other hand, was imperceptibly slowing down . . . Jamain was slowly but surely falling asleep . . . And the car was keeping its inexorable course! Within one or, at the most, two minutes Jamain would be in dreamland—and the Austin in the ditch . . . Boudier, who must already be puzzled by his slow speed, would turn round. But the cork had to be carried to the end of its mysterious voyage. Then, just in time, Ferblantine disappeared round a bend.

Jamain, almost unconscious, was slumped down in his seat. With a final reflex of the experienced driver, he put his foot on the brake.

The game had gone on long enough. Robert sat up straight, seized the wheel with one hand and switched off the engine. The Austin came to a halt on the grass at the roadside.

With difficulty he pulled Jamain from the driver's seat. The latter half-opened a glassy eye and grimaced.

"Wretched kid, you fooled me. Well, you won't . . ."

That was all he could say. He had fallen fast asleep.

Robert took his place at the wheel and restarted the engine. He had to follow Ferblantine and act temporarily as a substitute for Jamain so as not to arouse Boudier's suspicions. A thousand questions sprang to his mind but he did not puzzle over them. They could all wait. The first thing to do was find out what they planned to do with Ferblantine. Then everything would be made clear.

After the bend round which the coral Dauphine had disappeared, there was another straight stretch of road. Boudier, surprised at no longer seeing the Austin in the mirror, had slowed down and was only 500 yards ahead . . . "Let's hope he doesn't wait for us to catch up!" Robert thought. "If he does, I've had it!"

Luckily, Boudier, reassured by the sight of the Austin, set off again at a good speed. Robert prudently kept 300 yards behind. At that distance the other could not see what had happened.

The two cars turned on to the D 67 in the direction of Echouboulains. Robert smiled. He guessed where his involuntary guide was leading him . . . He saw they were coming to the track which had led them through the forest to the 67 after the events by the forester's lodge. Ferblantine turned up it . . . Robert followed—at a distance . . . Boudier was driving quite unsuspiciously. Robert let the distance between them widen. They were nearly there. A little path led off to the right. He turned up it, went on thirty yards or so and finally found what looked like a suitable place, a dense thicket with a good approach for a vehicle.

He left the path, slipped through the trees and with a last touch of the accelerator sent the Austin right in among the bushes.

Jamain's eyes were tight shut: he was sleeping like a log.

Robert ran through the forest. When he reached the edge of the little clearing in the middle of which stood the forester's lodge, he crouched behind a woodpile and looked round him.

Fifty yards from where he crouched stood Ferblantine, parked just behind a big American limousine with the lid of its boot wide open. Boudier was anxiously looking back in the direction from which the Austin should have come . . . Two other individuals were doing something inside Ferblantine. The doors hid their head and shoulders.

Robert covered ten yards at a bound and hid behind another woodpile. He heard Boudier fuming.

"What in hell's name is he doing?"

"Well, we've done our job," one of the men said.

"What *can* they be up to?" Robert wondered. Boudier had reached the house only five minutes at the most before himself. They hadn't had the time to do much!

The two men stood up and Robert nearly gave a cry of surprise when he recognized Jules Langlois. Jules, whose double he thought he had seen in this very spot only a few hours previously!

Taking even more care, he went closer.

"It's the right one this time?" Boudier asked.

"Sure, boss!" Jules answered. "We checked!"

"All right, get it in the car quick and buzz off," Boudier told him, and then returned to cursing "that ass Jamain".

"He may have got stuck," said Jules' companion, a great gawky, gangling creature.

Boudier was in no mood for conversation. He told the gawky chap to get moving.

"Put the other bundle in the Dauphine," he added. "It weights as much as a dead donkey."

The other two walked up to the house and calmly opened the door.

A minute later they reappeared, carrying a long bundle rolled up in a multi-coloured rug.

Robert gave a start. He had seen what stuck out of the end Jules was carrying—a pair of feet. A man! The bundle moved a fraction.

"He's beginning to wake up," commented Jules' assistant.

Boudier remarked that the parcel was so well tied there was no danger of its escaping.

The man was unceremoniously dumped on the floor of the American car, between the front and back seats, and covered up with another rug.

Boudier was growing more and more impatient.

"Hurry up and bring the other down," he shouted. "I'm going to try and find Jamain . . . You're to make for Paris as fast as you can. The boss is waiting for you. Go via Brie-Comte-Robert; the road won't be so busy. And watch out! Don't drive too fast . . . You're dumb enough to get pinched!"

The other two hung their heads and hurried off to bring out the other "package". But it had not been wrapped up. It was a limp, apparently lifeless body with a head lolling . . .

Robert had to bite his lips not to cry out.

It was Serge!

Serge was propped up on the front seat in Ferblantine.

Boudier had said: "I'm going to look for Jamain . . . " He would not find him, of course, but then what would he do? There was not a second to lose. Jules and his companion were still trying to sit Serge up in the seat . . . He gave them a lot of trouble, collapsing and tumbling over onto the driver's seat.

"Well, prop him up against the door then," exclaimed Boudier irritably.

Robert slipped silently out of the clearing, plunged into the forest and started to run. The Austin was not far off. As he reached it, he heard an engine start up. It was the American car. He was on tenterhooks, listening for the familiar roar of Ferblantine . . .

He had ceased to be the cork in the water. He now knew exactly what he wanted to do. The game had begun. He did not know all his opponent's cards; he did not even know what kind of game they were playing.

Boudier would be watching the American car drive off. It would soon reach the first turning in the direction of the D 213. This was it; he drove off . . .

Ferblantine was in second, chugging noisily up the muddy track. She was nearly there. Robert pulled the Austin's starter. The engine fired. He switched off, restarted her, switched off, restarted her and switched off a third time. Then he listened. Boudier had stopped on a level with the path. Obviously he had recognized the characteristic note of the little Austin's engine. Robert took out the ignition key and threw it as far as he could into the undergrowth. He then lifted up the bonnet and tore out the distributor leads.

"Hello! Boudier!" he called out. "I'm over here in the wood!"

He had not shouted: he had just called out in a disguised voice.

He heard Ferblantine's engine stop. The other

had switched off . . . So he had decided to risk a reconnaissance on foot, thought Robert happily. That would simplify matters.

He slipped silently in among the brushwood, taking care not to snap the branches, and started to make his way towards the track on a parallel with the path Boudier had taken. He heard him coming nearer . . . He kept on . . . Then the other's footsteps grew fainter . . . They had passed each other.

"What's the matter?" Boudier shouted.

He had seen the Austin and was addressing the sleeping Jamain.

Robert dashed off.

The coral Dauphine was in the middle of the track. Boudier had not even shut the door. In three strides Robert reached his car. Serge was fast asleep in his seat. He took his hand. It was quite cool: he did not seem to be ill. He was resting peacefully.

Robert got behind the wheel and saw the ignition key. He had expected to find that the thief had interfered with the wiring . . . But he had not needed to take that much trouble. He had a key!

In a flash Robert realized why he had noticed no trace of force having been used on the door handle when he surprised Jamain sitting in Ferblantine . . . These gentlemen had all they needed. This was sorcery . . . Then suddenly he started to laugh. What a fool he was! *Jules* was tied up with these people and had all the time in the world when he was in the garage to have another key cut!

He drove off. Dear Ferblantine.

Behind him, cries came from the undergrowth. Boudier had obviously realized that he'd been tricked . . .

Robert changed into second and accelerated.

He was 200 yards away from the path when he saw

in his mirror a little figure leaping up and down. So much for Boudier, the rat!

"And now," said Robert to his sleeping companion, "let's go and settle our account with Jules!"

❋ ❋ 15 ❋ ❋

ROBERT DAROUX WAS NO righter of wrongs. The only kind of adventure in which he was interested was a sports-car race. He had no taste for mysteries or punch-ups. He sensibly thought that the events in which he had just taken part were a matter for the police. It was up to them to answer the thousand questions that troubled him and to punish those who deserved it. In acting as he had done, he had followed a single goal: to recover Ferblantine and to snatch Serge from the hands of his abductors.

While watching Boudier, Jules and their assistant from his hiding place among the woodpiles, he had worked out a very simple plan for himself: "I'll pick up my pal and my car and I'll return to Villeneuve, Serge will be looked after, they'll take care of Boudier and his henchmen after I've said what they've done—and this time I've a drugged Serge as a piece of evidence. Then, I'll call the Crank and, if Serge wakes up, we'll finish the rally."

However, there was a fly in the ointment. And this fly was the man wrapped up in a tartan rug who had been loaded into the American car.

"He's beginning to wake up," Jules' mate had said with reference to that "package".

So it was not a corpse. Not yet, at any rate.

But people so set on destruction would not hesitate to eliminate someone who got in their way.

That man was in mortal danger. Robert jettisoned his original plan and set off as fast as he could up the Paris road in Jules' wake.

He knew that Jules was heading for the capital, where a mysterious "boss" was impatiently waiting for him. He would go through Brie-Comte-Robert, which he would take the N 19, as Boudier had ordered him to do. He had also warned him to drive at a reasonable speed. If he followed the route chosen by Boudier, Jules would be obliged to cover forty-three miles before he reached Paris. Robert decided to go via Le Châtelet-en-Brie and Melun on the N 5. The traffic would not be bad. It had been raining all day and there were not many people out on the road. So Robert estimated that he would gain some twelve miles on his quarry. He would turn off at Maisons-Alfort to rejoin the N 19. Then he would only have to wait for the American car to come by and follow it at a discreet distance.

Jules would have to stop some time, most probably at the big boss's house . . .

"It will be easy when I get to Paris," Robert said to himself. "I'll choose a crossroads where there is a policeman on point duty and block their way at the risk of a crumpled wing. Then the policeman can cope with Jules and his mate and the poor chap rolled up like a sausage!"

As he drove along, he gave an occasional glance at Serge. The latter was still sleeping peacefully, but was sitting a little more upright and looked less limp. As they passed through Melun, he gave a grunt. At

Villeneuve-Saint-Georges, he half-opened one eye and quickly closed it again.

Robert looked more and more frequently at his watch. It had been half past seven when he left the Villermoy forest . . . Now it said ten past eight. He had made good time. Sometimes, though, he felt a twinge of anxiety. Perhaps he had done wrong. Perhaps he should have stopped at the first police station and warned the authorities . . . Y-es, but think of the time it would have taken to convince the police! He had Serge as his living proof, but that was all . . . They'd have started to look at him askance . . . as the promotors of the rally had done in the afternoon. Besides, he did not know the American car's registration number; he hadn't been able to catch sight of it. He was not even sure of the make: was it a Dodge or a Chevrolet?

He reached the Avenue du Général-Leclerc at Maisons-Alfort and was back on to the N 19. He drove on for a few minutes, then noticed a street on his right. He went down it and turned so as to be ready to make a quick get-away. He parked some distance back from the junction: Jules would recognize Ferblantine from the number painted on her doors. He switched off and got out, after giving Serge a shake. The latter was still fighting against sleep but he was no longer in a coma.

Robert went and took up a position at the side of the avenue. He hid behind a parked van.

The cars went by in an almost unbroken double stream. Twice, Robert's heart beat faster . . . No, he was wrong . . . Jules' American car was not like that. Besides, the first contained a couple and the second a single middle-aged man.

Suddenly he saw it, fifty yards away. It was travelling at a steady speed in the second lane. He recognized

Jules and the giant. He ran to Ferblantine, started her up and drove up to the junction. He could still see the American car; it was past the junction. Ignoring the curses of the other drivers, he squeezed his way into the same lane.

Jules and the giant were not hurrying; they were carefully obeying Boudier's instructions. Carried along by the stream, both cars crossed the bridge at Charenton and entered Paris by the Porte de Bercy . . . Robert had prudently kept his distance, but now profited by the straight stretch along the Quai de la Rapee to get nearer. Next the American car took the Boulevard Diderot and drove past the Gare de Lyon. Its right winker came into action; it slowed down and drove majestically into the Garage du Soleil at the corner of the boulevard and the Avenue Daumesnil.

Robert had been copying Jules. He had slowed down on seeing the winker's orange eye blinking at him . . . He hurriedly tried to pass the car immediately ahead of him so that it would conceal Ferblantine from the people in the garage . . .

He was furious. He had let himself be caught napping like a half-wit. He had sheepishly followed the American car instead of forcing the issue. He could easily have caught up with Jules before he reached the Gare de Lyon . . . It was not as though there were a shortage of police in the area.

"What was he to do?"

"I'm going to park and tell my story to the first policeman I can find," he said to himself . . . "I've played the lone hero long enough!"

Robert continued down the Boulevard Diderot, turned right into the Rue Crozatier and right again into the Rue Abel-Leblanc. He wanted to get nearer to the Garage du Soleil . . . To come to think of it, that name rang a bell. Had it not been a director of the dump, a man called Mercier, who had tried to buy back Ferblantine?

A little black 4 CV passed him and stopped dead in front of his bonnet. Robert jammed on his brakes. He then wound down his window and put his head out to tell the clumsy fool what he thought of him. He opened his mouth but no sound came.

Two men had jumped out of the tiny car. They levelled two efficient looking sub-machine guns at Ferblantine.

"Hands up, both of you!" snapped one of them.

Robert suddenly realized that they were policemen. For reasons already made clear, he was delighted: this meeting removed thc necessity for a step he thought was going to be a difficult one. But his pleasure was tempered by the black muzzles of the tommy-guns. Particularly as the policeman aiming at Serge was growing annoyed. While Robert had prudently done as he was told, and shown by his attitude that he had no intention of fighting it out, his co-driver had not moved a muscle. Naturally: he was still asleep.

"Hands up! You, too! No funny business," the policeman shouted.

Seeing that the other had not budged—hc was probably up to some trick—and knowing that attack is the best method of defence, the policeman leaped forward and pulled open Ferblantine's right-hand door. Serge, whom Jules had lovingly propped up against that same door, lost his support and tumbled out onto the roadway.

The policeman jumped back, expecting some subtle judo hold, and again levelled his tommy-gun on the unfortunate young accountant.

The supposedly bellicose Serge yawned, opened his eyes, shut them, opened them again and gave a grunt.

In the meantime Robert had been hauled out of Ferblantine by the suspicious policeman's colleague.

"You've had it!" the man told him.

By now, Robert felt really rather anxious. He tried to smile amiably and searched wildly for the best way of telling his tale. He failed miserably and said dimly:

"I was looking for you."

"So were we!" answered the man of the law, laughing in his face.

A new character came on the scene; a police sergeant also had been sitting in the 4 CV.

"I've just got onto H.Q., he told his men. "The inspector's on his way."

Then, glancing at Serge, who was still lying in the road, he added:

"What's the matter with your mate?"

"They put him to sleep," Robert explained. "I don't think it can be serious; he seems to be coming to."

The sergeant pulled some handcuffs from his pockets.

"Put out your hands," he said in a friendly fashion.

Robert stiffened. All he got for cooperating with the police was a string of insults. The last time, when they had tried to steal Ferblantine, the police had wanted to throw him into jail.

He protested vehemently.

"*I* haven't done anything," he exclaimed. "I came to Paris to get you to arrest these characters who'd tied up a chap . . . I'm no criminal . . ."

The policeman standing beside him grabbed his arm roughly.

"Put out your hands," the sergeant said. "You can talk to the inspector!"

Robert was forced to proffer his wrists. The bracelets snapped to with a sharp click that made him shudder.

He was too shattered to speak. What was the use of arguing? Perhaps he would manage to explain to the inspector.

A small crowd gathered and was told to move on. They did so, grumbling. Then a police-car siren wailed down a nearby street.

"There they are!" said the sergeant. (He was not that dumb).

Two minutes later the police van pulled up behind Ferblantine. It was followed by a black saloon.

Two men in plain clothes got out of it. One of them had a bandaged hand. Robert glanced at him, then looked again. It was absurd, impossible, unthinkable —but his eyes did not deceive him.

"Monsieur Barbier!" he cried.

Barbier—it was indeed he—had a shock when he recognized Robert Daroux. The sight of a Martian would have surprised him less.

"Well I'm damned! . . . Robert Daroux! What are you doing here?"

Suddenly his face darkened and grew severe.

"What has been going on?" he asked the sergeant.

"We received a call from H.Q. only ten minutes ago . . . They told us to follow the Dauphine, stop it and guard its occupants . . . There were only these two on board. One of them's sleeping like a log: he seems to have been drugged."

Barbier turned to Robert.

"I suppose there has been a misunderstanding . . . How did you get here?"

Level-headed though he was, Monsieur Daroux's eldest boy began to feel anger mounting within him In the first place, what was he, Barbier, playing at? What was a travelling salesman doing with the police? And why had he disappeared with Rambaud, the Crank, Jean and all the others? He would like an explanation. And how about these handcuffs? Did he he think it was amusing for a respectable young man to be treated like a highway robber?

This outburst hypnotized the policeman, who stood frowning.

Barbier did not appear to be upset.

"It's true," he said, "I owe you an explanation . . . and my apologies," he added, when the sergeant had freed Robert. "May I introduce myself: Chief Inspector Barbier of the Customs Department. I'm a colleague of your friend Rambaud's."

"Rambaud! So he doesn't sell underwear!"

"No . . . Now, let's have your story and try to unravel this mess."

Robert meekly agreed. He recounted his skirmishes with Boudier and Jamain, how he had recovered Serge and Ferblantine, and why he had come to Paris, abandoning the rally.

"You see," he explained, "they threw a bound man into their car . . . I said to myself: if I tell you my story, that poor chap may be dead before anyone believes me . . . I'll catch up with them in Paris and cause an accident. But they escaped under my nose: they drove into a garage, the Garage du Soleil!"

"What!" yelled Barbier. "Are you sure?"

"As sure as I'm standing here."

Barbier turned towards the man in plain clothes who accompanied him and had not said a word.

"They've fooled us! . . . We were expecting a coral Dauphine."

"What is the make of this car?" the superintendent asked Robert.

"A Chevvy or a Dodge."

The superintendent took a notebook out of his pocket and flipped through it.

"I made a note," he said, "8.31: arrival of a Dodge,

registration number 4532 FY75. It's on our list. It belongs to one of the garage's customers . . ."

"They must have borrowed it," murmured Barbier thoughtfully. "I'm beginning to get it. If Robert hadn't tailed the Dodge we'd have been had for suckers. Superintendent, we must search the garage at once . . . There's a man there in mortal danger."

"I've a blank warrant," the superintendent said . . . "Have you any idea of the identity of the man they've taken?"

"I'm afraid it may be Rambaud."

"Monsieur Rambaud!" exclaimed Robert, who had been following every word. "How on earth . . .?"

"I don't know," Barbier answered. "We'll find out soon."

He stopped talking and looked at the young man reflectively.

"If you could come with us," he went on, "it would help a lot . . . You might be able to identify the people who attacked you in the wood. We are familiar with a good number of them, but you never know . . ."

Then he turned to the superintendent and added:

"Detail two men to look after the Dauphine. They can take Monsieur Daroux's friend to a chemist's . . ."

While Robert and Barbier were sorting things out, Serge, who had been more or less forgotten, opened his eyes, yawned and stared in owlish amazement at the mass of uniforms. He painfully sat up and leaned back against Ferblantine. At last he spotted his friend. At that moment, Barbier gave orders for someone to look after him . . .

"Hey!" Serge said to Robert. "What's happening? Have we had an accident?"

Robert ran over.

"No, it's O.K. How are you feeling?"

"All right . . . I certainly slept . . . It has made me quite dizzy!"

Gradually his memory of what had hit him began to come back.

"What exactly did happen to me? . . . I spoke to the Crank on the phone. Then I fell into a pit . . . Where are we?"

Barbier reassured him. It was all going to be all right. Serge had not sufficiently recovered to argue. He did not insist. Two agents helped him on to the back seat of the Dauphine.

"Are you letting her go like that?" the superintendent said to Barbier, pointing at the car. "That's not according to regulations."

The inspector swept aside the objection with a gesture.

"Our birds have been cleverer than I thought," he said. "We won't find anything. Besides . . ."

While he had been speaking he had opened the driver's door. He bent down and carefully examined the steel tubes supporting the seat.

"Just what I thought," he said. "They've changed the seat . . . Rambaud had made a mark on it. He showed it to me this morning . . ."

"For Pete's sake!" exclaimed Robert. "What IS it all about?"

Serge, on the other hand, just nodded. He had given up trying to understand.

"I'll tell you later," Barbier said.

Two policemen got into Ferblantine. One of them took the wheel. They set off for the nearest chemist's. The men from the police van got back into their vehicle.

"Let's go!" said Barbier, dragging Robert and the superintendent off towards the black saloon.

The superintendent ordered the driver to go ahead of the van.

"Be careful," he said. "He's going to stop at the corner of the Rue Guillaume . . . then we drive to the Garage du Soleil. You'll go in and the van will follow us."

The superintendent turned to Barbier.

"It's no good asking for reinforcements," he explained. "My four men from the Rue Guillaume will watch the garage's emergency exits. We have about half a dozen left. They'll be enough: Mercier and his gang won't suspect anything. We'll come down on them like a thunderbolt!"

He smiled at Robert.

"As for you, Monsieur Daroux, there's nothing for you to do. You'll stay with the driver . . ."

Robert nodded. He had no wish to tangle with Mercier and his men. He glanced furtively at his watch. Nine-fifteen!

In an hour's time the loud-speakers would call on the Daroux-Rivois team to come up to the starting line for the night-time section. He felt a twinge of annoyance. This incomprehensible business was going to make him lose his first rally. And they weren't so badly placed.

The black saloon screeched to a halt.

The van, which was just behind them, stopped dead so as to block the door . . . Robert felt he was watching a thriller. Doors slammed. Barbier and the superintendent leaped out of the car. Policemen armed with tommy-guns clattered up with a rattle of hobnail boots. A man wearing green overalls, obviously on duty at the pumps, was stuck up against the wall. Robert saw Barbier and the superintendent run up some stairs. Each held a black object in his hand. A number of police followed them. There were shouts and a succession of sharp commands. There was a thunder of feet on the first floor, then silence.

The superintendent's driver, who knew it all by heart, gave a yawn.

"The show's over," he said. "With a bit of luck I'll soon be able to take my wife to the cinema. I promised I would. The last performance. They're showing a psychological thriller . . ."

Barbier appeared at the head of the staircase, unfamiliar with his bandaged head that made him look like an Indian.

"Robert," he shouted. "Come here, please, we need you!"

❋ ❋ 16 ❋ ❋

JACQUES RAMBAUD, CHIEF INSPECTOR of Customs, stretched luxuriously, stubbed out his cigarette and sat down. He cast a weary but satisfied look round him. The exhaustion and strain of this mad day showed in his face.

They were in the director's office in the Garage du Soleil. Sitting in a row against the wall, each with handcuffs on his wrists and hangdog expressions, were Gaston Mercier, Jules Langlois, Philippe Dorien, a lanky creature with a sly air, and the petrol-pump attendant.

Seated opposite them, but in armchairs, were Robert Daroux and Serge Rivois, now wide awake, waiting with curiosity to see what would happen.

Superintendent Maurin, standing by the window with Barbier, said:

"Well, that's all tied up, Inspector. The police van should be here any minute."

Jerking his head towards Robert and Serge, he added:

"These young men might as well accompany us.

We'll take down their statement. Tomorrow is Sunday and . . ."

It was apparent that the superintendent wanted to have the case off his hands as soon as possible. In any event he was not directly concerned. He had only come into it to assist the others. These Customs officers could figure it all out. Once he'd filled in all the forms to cover his concern in the business, he would wash his hands of it.

Rambaud absent-mindedly expressed his agreement.

"Now that we have covered all the ground," he said, "and your statements have enabled us to clear up one or two doubtful points, I should like to thank you. It is thanks to you that I've been able to bring my investigation to a successful conclusion. It is also thanks to you (here Rambaud smiled) that tomorrow morning I shall be able to sleep late and take my time over my coffee and croissants. If you had not intervened, Robert, I certainly should have had no further occasion to enjoy breakfast. The dead have no worries. True, Mercier?"

The latter shrugged his shoulders.

"We didn't mean to hurt you," he mumbled.

Scarlet with embarrassment, Robert scratched his neck and murmured.

"I only did my duty. I didn't know you were the unconscious body Jules was carrying . . . I must admit I don't understand much about this business . . . It seems to be some sort of illegal traffic . . ."

"Yes, how did *we* become involved in it?" Serge asked.

Rambaud got up and lit a cigarette.

"It's true," he said. "Up to now you have only seen certain sides of the business. I do owe you an explanation. So here goes:

"You are probably aware that the Customs and Excise Department includes in addition to the uniformed officer you find at every border post, station or airport, inspectors entrusted with shall we say, more delicate tasks. Barbier and I belong to this service . . . Some months ago we learned that diamond merchants in Paris had been offered rough diamonds brought into the country illegally. I will spare you the details of an enquiry which led to my coming to this conclusion. The hub of this traffic was the Garage du Soleil. But how could I prove it? And, above all, how could I catch Mercier and his gang on the job? I might, if worse had come to worst, have intercepted a secret consignment, but these people are so clever that I would risk warning them without putting a stop to things. I therefore set out to make a systematic survey of the comings and goings of the people working in the garage. I investigated each of them pretty thoroughly. For example, I discovered that Jules Langlois was betting heavily and leading a life that would not be possible merely on his wages as a mechanic. He was earning something outside his regular job . . . A few weeks ago, Jules disappeared. The policeman detailed to keep an eye on him reported that he had managed to get himself a job at the Garage de l'Avenir in Le Plessis. My first reaction was to think that the gang had set up a new headquarters. I watched the garage . . . You know Monsieur Médor. After we had been talking for only five minutes, he told me about the attack on the Crank three days previously and about the theft of the seat. There were two alternatives: either the Crank was one of Mercier's accomplices, or Jules had come to the Garage de l'Avenir for a particular reason. The theft of the seat naturally drew my attention to the car. I made inquiries: I learned—what you know, incidentally—that its previous owner, a man named Gavard, was usually resident in Switzerland, where he worked for one of the international organizations. Switzerland was the distribution point for the traffic in uncut diamonds: Interpol was sure of that. Further enquiries enabled us to conclude that Mercier was using several of his clients' cars for his traffic. The plan was an extremely simple one: his customers were also customers of Gavard's garage in Geneva. Without their knowledge, the Swiss traffikers would hide the package they wanted to send in an agreed place in the upholstery. Mercier would retrieve it in Paris. If the Customs should discover the package—which was unlikely, as the customers were known to be respectable people who regularly crossed the border at the same spot, so the Customs would not make a detailed examination of their cars—their inquiries would reach a dead end . . . Mercier and his accomplices were taking practically no risk at all.

We might know the channel of operation, but we were not much nearer catching the villains—until chance dealt us a trump card: Ferblantine! The smugglers in Geneva must have hidden a package in the car which, as a result of Gavard's accident, had fallen into Bricard's hands. That explained the theft of the seat. The diamonds must be inside! Only the thief, surprised by Robert, made a mistake . . . He took the wrong one! Mercier dropped strong-arm methods and sent Jules to try and retrieve his property by gentler means . . ."

"Now I understand why Jules said that one of his friends was trying to get hold of a Dauphine seat!" Robert exclaimed.

"And why," Serge put in, "when he learned we had put the original seat in Ferblantine, because the one the scrap dealer gave us was stained, he lost interest. But why didn't he just steal it?"

"Mercier was determined that the business should be carried out without any fuss," Rambaud explained. "He was afraid that the theft of a second seat would rouse the suspicions of the police. Particularly, you must remember, as the seat with the diamonds in it was in Robert's bedroom. Its disappearance would have been bound to give rise to speculation!"

"But Mercier was wrong", cut in Jules, shooting a nasty look at his boss. "He was so sharp he cut himself . . . And to think of the weeks I spent jackassing around at Le Plessis!"

"Shut your face!" shouted Mercier. "If you think you're going to get clear by crawling to the police you've got another think coming!"

The pair were interrupted by the telephone bell.

Everyone's eyes turned to the instrument.

"It must be headquarters," said the superintendent, stretching out his hand to pick up the receiver.

Robert leaped into the air.

"Wait! . . . Suppose it's Boudier. By now, he must have repaired the distributor . . ."

"He's right," agreed Rambaud, who then turned to Jules. "If you do as you're told," he said to him, "things won't go too hard with you . . . You're going to answer the phone. If it is Boudier, you're to tell him that Mercier's orders are that he is to return as fast as he can to the garage . . . O.K.?"

Jules hesitated.

"You wouldn't do that!" his boss exploded.

The superintendent silenced him with a threatening gesture.

Jules went miserably over to the telephone, and picked up the receiver. Rambaud had taken the spare ear-phone.

"Hello?"

"Who's that?" asked a nasal voice at the other end of the line.

"It's Jules."

"Get Mercier. It's me, Boudier. I've got some bad news!"

"Mercier says you're to come back, and Jamain, too . . ."

"I wanted to explain to him. That kid, Robert, tricked us. He's gone off with the Dauphine and his pal who is still asleep. He wrecked the distributor . . ."

Rambaud, who knew exactly what had happened to Boudier, signed to Jules to cut it short. The mechanic obeyed.

"That's your lookout," he said. "Mercier's orders are for you to get back here."

"All right," the other answered. "We're on the Paris road. After what happened we didn't return to the rally!"

"See you soon then," Jules said and hung up.

Barbier and the superintendent began to laugh.

"That's it, 'see him soon!' You couldn't have put it better," the inspector remarked.

Rambaud turned to Mercier, who was fuming in the corner.

"Cool off!" he said, "We'd have caught your little friends in any case; they wouldn't have got far. Jules just saved us a bit of trouble! Thanks," he added, turning to Robert. "You've got a flair! You'd make a good detective."

Robert answered in pantomime that he really didn't have the vocation.

Rambaud went on with his story.

"We therefore decided to watch Ferblantine closely so as to be able to grab anyone who made off with the car, that's to say, the diamonds concealed in her. Then came the day when you first took her out on the road. I must admit that Mercier and his men nearly outsmarted us. We didn't think they'd go into action so quickly. It was fortunate that luck and Gendarme Tropinet were on our side! Nevertheless, that incident served to bring me into closer touch with your little team. You can now understand my sudden enthusiasm for motor rallies . . . I never let you out of my sight, you, Jules or the car. Then the great day dawned . . . I had a feeling that the gang would take advantage of the rally to try something. That was why I took Barbier with me. Our plan was a simple one. We didn't dream that Mercier would attempt anything so spectacular during the running. All it needed was for us to watch what happened at the end of each section. You had only just left when we realized we had made a mistake. Serge must have told you how Rosalie was sabotaged and Barbier attacked . . ."

"I gave him a brief outline just now," Serge said. "The Crank told me over the phone a few minutes ago. You should have heard him!" he exclaimed, turning to Robert. "He had to leave Rosalie at Tournan and come back in the van with Adèle and your brother . . . If he catches one of these gentlemen, they'll know about it!"

"Did you tell him about the episode of the forester's lodge and the motorcyclist?" asked Robert.

"I hadn't the time. He hung up."

"I was just coming to that," continued Rambaud. "Barbier and I left the Crank at Tournan. I was worried about my friend's condition and I had to make a new plan. I presumed that Mercier would soon go into the attack . . . I could still thwart him. Barbier got the local police doctor to look at him. He just had a nasty crack on the head, that was all. He could manage. I gave him the job of watching the Garage du

Soleil and contacting the nearest police station . . . Then, I left my own car, which the villains had spotted, and took Barbier's Aronde. I then drove to Seine-et-Marne, after phoning through to the various controls set up along the route by the promoters of the rally. I learned that you were still somewhere on the route, so I had a chance to join in the hunt and catch Mercier and his men red-handed. If I failed, it meant that the gang would have managed to capture Ferblantine. It was a mathematical certainty that they would drive her to the Garage du Soleil to retrieve their diamonds.

"I did think of doing that," Mercier muttered, "but only for a minute. I was afraid of attracting attention. It was those numbers painted on the doors . . ."

"Why were you so sure that something would happen during the competition?" Robert asked.

"Adèle had said in my hearing that she had recognized one of the men in the Austin which started after you. She had seen him at the garage. When I heard this, I thought of the character in the Aronde who came to Le Plessis to try and get the seat back. It was only after he failed that Jules came into the running."

"The big lanky chap came, too," Serge said. "I told you. He had a D.S. 19."

"You had a narrow escape that day!" replied Rambaud. "I have a feeling that if I hadn't turned up, you would really have been done for . . ."

The awkward giant opened his mouth to protest. The inspector silenced him by remarking that it was surprising he had pretended not to recognize Jules, his accomplice.

"Not that it matters. The main thing is that no damage was done. Whatever your intentions were, that is not why you are under arrest."

Rambaud went on with his story:

"I therefore waited at Châtelet-en-Brie. I saw Ferblantine pass. You were at the wheel. All was going well. So far Mercier had not tried anything. The Austin arrived five minutes after you . . . I followed it at a safe distance . . . Suddenly I saw it turn up the forest track. I was sufficiently familiar with the rally course to know that this was no part of it . . . There was something fishy going on. I followed up that track . . . and you can guess what happened then . . ."

"So it was you, the driver we saw grappling with those two characters!" exclaimed Robert.

"Yes, it was me. The others had spotted me. Like an idiot I dashed up to their car. Seeing it was abandoned, I got out of my own—and the Boudier-Jamain team went for me tooth and nail!"

"Boudier-Jamain!" cried Serge.

"Yes, of course. The rain and the distance concealed their identity."

"They had oilskins on!" said Robert. "And we were too het up to think of identifying people whom, incidentally, we hadn't seen at the start."

Turning to Jules, he asked:

"What was the meaning of that masquerade, with the motorcyclist and the ambush in the undergrowth?"

Jules grimaced. The marmoset was looking very sad and shamefaced.

"I knew the forester's lodge and that corner of the forest. It was I who suggested the plan. I was sure you wouldn't try to cross the pool right away, that you would look for another route when you saw wheel marks on the other side of the water. The thing was to make you get out of the car . . . That's why we put the tree across the path. In the meantime my pals were going to change the seat in Ferblantine. I was hiding behind a pile of logs watching you . . . And I had to sneeze—well, you know that! You got scared and we lost our chance! When Boudier saw you making a dash for it, he told us to forget security and catch you . . . But you managed to escape."

"But they got my number!" said Rambaud. "They searched me and found my Customs Officer's Identity Card. They forced me to drink some muck after leaving me in the forester's lodge. They had decided to deal with me later."

"What happened then?" asked Serge.

"Jules will tell us," Rambaud said with a laugh. "He's longing to talk . . . But you'd best watch it, my friend: if you try and fool us, I can guess enough to cut you down to size."

Jules related the sequel without too much pressure. The two boys' dash had shaken Jamain and his accomplices somewhat. The appearance of a Customs inspector worried them. Boudier, the most energetic of them, decided to go with his co-driver to Villeneuve to see how Robert and Serge had reacted. When they got there, they found that all was well . . . The president of the Automobile Club took them aside to ask if they had seen a motorcyclist and had been led astray. Naturally they said they had not. No one took the two boys seriously. Boudier immediately thought up a new plan. With the ignition key Jules had made, they would merely take Ferblantine. They followed Robert and Serge and heard them ask for a telephone call.

Boudier rushed to the control and got the announcer to ask for Robert. Serge, when he had gone off to answer the telephone, couldn't then keep an eye on the car. But the car was hemmed in by a parked D.S. 19.

The D.S. went off eventually but by then precious time had been lost. Nevertheless Jamain tried his luck. And at that moment Robert appeared.

Boudier had come back from the control and was supervising operations from the inside of the café. When he saw Robert come in, he realized that again the plan had misfired. So he changed his tactics. He went to the telephone, calmly hit Serge over the head and slung him over his shoulder like a sack of potatoes. As a precaution, he had ordered Jules and the giant, Dorier, to post themselves with their car, the big American job, at the back gate opening on to the countryside. He handed them Serge to take to the forester's lodge. His new plan was quite clear. It consisted of kidnapping Robert, who was more vulnerable now he was on his own, and driving him in Ferblantine into the forest. The substitute seat for the Dauphine was in the Dodge's boot. They would change them over in peace and quiet. As for the two unconscious boys, they would leave them in the forest with the car after liberally sprinkling them with Scotch. Everyone would think they had decided to celebrate Robert's victory in the handling test and had got blind drunk. They could tell any story they liked; no one would believe them—particularly as all would be in order and Ferblantine present and correct!

"What do you think of that?" exclaimed Rambaud when Jules had finished.

"It's incredible!" said Serge.

"Were the diamonds actually in the seat?" Robert asked.

"We found the seat slashed open in the Dodge's boot. The diamonds were in Mercier's desk when we entered. It was the best catch *in flagrante delictu* of my whole career."

Outside they heard the wail of a siren.

"That's the prison van," said the superintendent, and added, for the benefit of Mercier and his accomplices, "They're spoiling you! You're going to have two motorcyclists as escort!"

Robert got up. The tall dark skinny boy stood awkwardly in the middle of the room.

"I suppose Serge and I will have to go with you," he said to Rambaud, "to make an official statement . . ."

"If you're tired, you can go home," the inspector offered. "We can deal with that tomorrow morning."

Robert shrugged his shoulders.

"No, we might as well get it over. In any case, we've plenty of time. We're out of the rally."

Serge gave a sigh that would break a heart of stone. "Do you realize, Monsieur Rambaud, that Robert went round in four minutes, nineteen point one seconds! He told me . . . while you were questioning the others . . . There was no reason why we shouldn't have got a good place in the night section. We'd have finished in the first five."

Suddenly, as though by magic, Chief Customs Inspector Rambaud turned back into plain Monsieur Rambaud, the underwear salesman and keen new rally-goer.

He whistled through his teeth:

"Four minutes nineteen point one seconds! I saw the plan of the course: that's really something!"

"Better than Roncier who won the Tour!"

"What a day!" Robert sighed. "We were all so happy this morning at Tournan. The Crank must be fuming! . . . So must my parents!"

Inspector Barbier interrupted him. "The truth is," he exclaimed, "that you couldn't care less about all this diamond-smuggling nonsense. All you're interested in is sport . . . Perhaps you don't realize that you have the right to a reward: a small percentage of the price of the diamonds you've helped us to recover!"

"And there's my skin!" exclaimed Rambaud. "I value it very highly and it was Robert who saved it. That's worth an extra prize!"

He winked at the two boys.

"I wouldn't be surprised if sooner or later I didn't see you start off on a rally at the wheel of an Alfa-Romeo . . . It sometimes pays to perform a service to society!"

"As much as that," murmured Serge—without appearing unduly excited.

Robert merely said that it would be very nice. Obviously the news, although he was pleased by it, did not console him for the ruined rally.

"These young people are insatiable!" joked the superintendent.

Rambaud was thinking. He glanced at his watch. It said a quarter past ten . . .

"Even if you were at Villeneuve," he said quietly, "you couldn't start. You must be worn out. You haven't had a bite of solid food since this morning . . ."

"But I'm fit as a fiddle!" Serge protested. "I've slept all day. I don't know what kind of drug they gave me but I feel fine. A nice big sandwich and a cup of coffee and I could go on for two nights without sleep!"

"I'm perfectly fit, too," echoed Robert. "If it's your first rally you go on to the bitter end. Even if I'd had to end by pushing Ferblantine, I'd have got there."

"The Crank's the one who's going to be disappointed."

"We have been dreaming of this day for years," said Robert. "So has Serge . . ."

Suddenly he made up his mind.

"Look, Monsieur Rambaud," he said, "perhaps we could try and get to Villeneuve? It isn't as though we had done anything. You can't stop us leaving."

"It's out of the question," the inspector exclaimed. "I don't want your deaths on my conscience! You were supposed to start at eleven, weren't you? Well, even if you were to drive like madmen, you'd get to Villeneuve too late. Covering over thirty-seven miles in forty minutes including driving through the suburbs just isn't possible!"

Rambaud was right. The two boys sadly dropped their heads.

The door opened and a motorcycle policeman appeared. The Black Maria was waiting. Mercier and his accomplices were led away.

Robert noticed that Barbier had dragged his friend and the superintendent off into a corner of the office. They were all three talking animatedly in whispers. The superintendent was getting worked up and protesting.

"I'll be responsible," Rambaud said aloud. "It's a good idea of Barbier's."

The superintendent shrugged his shoulders with a fatalistic air and left the room. They heard him tell a policeman to fetch the two motorcyclists. They arrived and all five began a fresh consultation. Robert and Serge looked on indifferently. Snatches of conversation reached them:

". . . a personal service . . . if the super agrees, we'll do it . . ." From time to time the motorcyclists glanced out of the corner of their eyes in the two boys' direction.

The little group separated. The policemen were smiling and looking rather pleased with themselves.

"All right," said Rambaud, "you're going back to Villeneuve . . ." (He looked at his watch. It was twenty-two minutes past ten.) "These gentlemen," he said, pointing to the patrolmen, "will clear the road for you. You'll drive like V.I.Ps!"

Robert and Serge stared open-mouthed at the motorcyclists, Rambaud, Barbier and the superintendent.

"My name's Ferrier," said one of the helmeted men, stretching out a hand. "This is my partner, Grignon . . . Have you ever driven like this before?"

Robert shook his head.

"I didn't imagine so. Chief Inspector Rambaud says you're a champion at the wheel. You'll be all right. Grignon will clear the road a hundred yards ahead. I'll ride between you both. Keep your eyes open!"

He laughed and added:

"One false move and we'll be in the ditch . . . And I've a wife and two kids!"

"But thirty-five minutes to do over thirty-seven miles!" protested Serge.

"Don't worry!" Rambaud cut in. "Off you go at once. I'm going to phone through to Villeneuve and ask them to send you off last. That will give you an extra quarter of an hour . . ."

Two minutes previously, the two boys could have posed for a statuary group entitled, "Castor and Pollux in despair." Rambaud's offer had transformed them like a magic wand.

"Well, are we going? cried Serge.

"We sure are!" said Robert.

"Let's go then!" chorused the two motorcyclists, amused at their transformation.

They dashed to the door. As they reached it, Robert turned round.

"Monsieur Rambaud, I still have just one more request: would you phone the Crank and tell him all's going well—*very* well!"

With that he dived down the stairs after the others.

The superintendent and the two inspectors stood

motionless, listening. Down below in the garage there were three bursts of thunder: the low growl of the police B.M.Ws. and the angry roar of Ferblantine, soon mingling with the howling of the sirens.

The noise reached a fantastic pitch and for a few seconds filled the avenue. Then it lessened, died away and finally ceased.

The motorcyclists and the boys were off on their race against time.

"What it is to be young!" sighed the superintendent.

He thought gloomily of his youth and of the administrative chaos he had created for himself by sending the two policemen down into Seine-et-Marne.

"I hope they get there in time," said Barbier.

Rambaud picked up the telephone . . .

"They're nice boys," he said. "I'd be very sorry if our sordid cops-and-robbers stuff stopped their dream coming true . . ."

It had rained for most of the day but it was a lovely evening. The stars glittered in the sky . . . Casual strollers were out enjoying at last the first feeling of summer.

Suddenly out of the night came the strident note of first one—then another siren; whistles blew their piercing blasts.

Two men in black, horsemen of a modern Apocalypse, flashed by ahead of a coral Dauphine.

By the time people had looked up they were gone, swallowed up by the darkness.

❋ ❋ 17 ❋ ❋

THE DAY DAWNED IN long milky streaks . . . At the entrance to Tournan-en-Brie, under a banner whose heavy black letters spelled out:

RALLYE DE LA BRIE – – ARRIVÉE

over 200 people were waiting. Competitors and fans . . .

A car emerged from the mist and crossed the line. A hoarse voice called out a time and a number . . . Sitting in a tent, their eyes swollen with lack of sleep, the judges crouched over the papers, working out the averages and index of performance . . . The hands of stop-watches were nibbling away the seconds and the minutes. Suddenly a shout went up:

"They're here!"

Two hundred necks were craned. Down the road headlights were looming out of the darkness. The crowd pressed forward and into the roadway . . . Now they could make out the car: the driver had dimmed his headlights. It was a coral Dauphine. It was almost there.

"It's them, all right!" someone yelled.

The Dauphine was already coming to a standstill. It

seemed to be engulfed in the human tide lapping round it.

"Give them a chance to get out," a voice called out.

And the people pressing round the car stood back a pace. The doors opened and the two boys emerged. For ten whole seconds they just stood there, motionless. Their faces were drawn and their eyes red with fatigue. They were swaying, dizzy from the road, the twists and turns leaping up at them out of the darkness, and from the constant roar of the engine . . .

A little bald man rushed up to one of the boys whose eyelids fluttered as he shook himself out of the weariness that enveloped him.

"Monsieur Bricard!" he stuttered.

The Crank was laughing and crying and hugging his champion . . .

"I came," he hiccuped. "We're . . . all . . . here . . .!"

There were fresh cries.

"Jean! And Monsieur Rambaud! And Barbier has come, too! . . . Mum! . . . Dad!"

Madame Daroux started sobbing on her eldest's shoulder. They were blocking the road. They were all talking at once. The rest of the world did not exist for the band from the Rue Bon-Repos . . .

"Monsieur Rambaud brought us," Jean explained. "He came and picked us up in his car, which the police at Châtelet-en-Brie had found hidden in a thicket . . ."

Monsieur Barbier took the Crank and Adèle in his Aronde.

Adèle Bricard pointed at her husband and said to Serge, "It made him ill! What a day it's been!"

The president of the Automobile Club and the judges elbowed their way through to the group. They were determined to shake hands with the boys. Monsieur Rambaud had said how wonderfully they had behaved. It was such an incredible affair! That was why they hadn't believed them!

"You should have seen Boudier's face when he arrived at the Garage du Soleil! He literally fell into the arms of the police officers waiting for him. He couldn't believe it!"

"What about Jamain?"

"He didn't wake up until he got to headquarters. He was amazement incarnate!"

"My friends," shouted the president [he had got up on to a chair so as to stand above the crowd and was holding a sheet of paper in his hand], "we are now in a position to announce the results of the 6th Brie Rally. Bur first I wish, both personally and on behalf of the promoters, to express my regret at a series of distressing —er—incidents that have upset the course of the competition. These—er—incidents have almost certainly robbed two of our latest recruits, the youngest members of our great sporting family, of a resounding victory . . . We are sure that they will have their revenge. Here, then, is the general classification: First, the Roncier-Dulac team who are also first in their own class. Second: Robert Daroux and Serge Rivois who are likewise first in their own class for cars under 1,000 c.c."

The president was unable to go on for the thunderous applause. Roncier, the champion, came up to Robert and Serge.

"I've just heard of your adventures," he said. "I am really sorry to win like this."

"Don't worry," cried Serge. "We're delighted. Don't be sorry about *anything*! We didn't hope for such a result. We've got an awful lot to learn."

The champion smiled as he turned to the Crank.

"Bravo, Bricard," he said. "Your boys will go far. Cool heads and warm hearts . . . I saw young Robert on that test . . . He's an ace! You can see he comes from a good school!"

The Crank went scarlet with pleasure. His cup was full.

"Robert and Serge will get a pretty big reward," Rambaud whispered to him. "You can think of getting them a racing car . . . That is your plan, isn't it? To climb the ladder up to the racetrack?"

The two boys heard him.

"We'll have to wait a bit yet," Robert said, and Serge agreed. "We've first got to do our basic training! And we'll do that in Ferblantine. She's the result of all our work and research. In a way she's everybody's baby. And you don't part with your first child just like that . . ."

Everybody smiled.

Day was breaking. A ray of sunlight appeared between two clouds, slid across the countryside and came to rest on the Dauphine's grimy body. Her chrome began to twinkle. Ferblantine, heroic under her mantle of mud, was smiling towards the future.

MADE AND PRINTED IN GREAT BRITAIN
BY CHARLES BIRCHALL & SONS, LTD.,
LIVERPOOL AND LONDON